THE LOOT OF CITIES,

AND FURTHER ADVENTURES

IN CRIME AND MYSTERY

THE LOOT OF CITIES,

AND FURTHER ADVENTURES IN CRIME AND MYSTERY

Arnold Bennett

COACHWHIP PUBLICATIONS

Landisville, Pennsylvania

Contents

THE LOOT OF CITIES:
THE ADVENTURES OF A MILLIONAIRE
IN SEARCH OF JOY

THE FIRE OF LONDON

Pensa, lettor, se quel che qui s'inizia
non procedesse, come tu avresti
di piu sapere angosciosa carizia.
　　　　　　—Dante.

I

"You're wanted on the telephone, sir."

Mr. Bruce Bowring, managing director of the Consolidated Mining and Investment Corporation, Limited (capital two millions, in one-pound shares, which stood at twenty-seven-and-six), turned and gazed querulously across the electric-lit spaces of his superb private office at the confidential clerk who addressed him. Mr. Bowring, in shirt-sleeves before a Florentine mirror, was brushing his hair with the solicitude of a mother who has failed to rear most of a large family.

"Who is it?" he asked, as if that demand for him were the last straw but one. "Nearly seven on Friday evening!" he added, martyrised.

"I think a friend, sir."

The middle-aged financier dropped his gold-mounted brush and, wading through the deep pile of the Oriental carpet, passed into the telephone-cabinet and shut the door.

"Hallo!" he accosted the transmitter, resolved not to be angry with it. "Hal*lo!* Are you there? Yes, I'm Bowring. Who are you?"

9

"*Nrrrr*," the faint, unhuman voice of the receiver whispered in his ear. "*Nrrrr. Cluck.* I'm a friend."

"What name?"

"No name. I thought you might like to know that a determined robbery is going to be attempted to-night at your house in Lowndes Square, a robbery of cash—and before nine o'clock. *Nrrrr.* I thought you might like to know."

"Ah!" said Mr. Bowring to the transmitter.

The feeble exclamation was all he could achieve at first. In the confined, hot silence of the telephone-cabinet this message, coming to him mysteriously out of the vast unknown of London, struck him with a sudden sick fear that perhaps his wondrously organised scheme might yet miscarry, even at the final moment. Why that night of all nights? And why before nine o'clock? Could it be that the secret was out, then?

"Any further interesting details?" he inquired, bracing himself to an assumption of imperturbable and gay coolness.

But there was no answer. And when after some difficulty he got the exchange-girl to disclose the number which had rung him up, he found that his interlocutor had been using a public call-office in Oxford Street. He returned to his room, donned his frock-coat, took a large envelope from a locked drawer and put it in his pocket, and sat down to think a little.

At that time Mr. Bruce Bowring was one of the most famous conjurers in the City. He had begun, ten years earlier, with nothing but a silk hat; and out of that empty hat had been produced, first the Hoop-La Limited, a South African gold-mine of numerous stamps and frequent dividends, then the Hoop-La No. 2 Limited, a mine with as many reincarnations as Buddha, and then a dazzling succession of mines and combination of mines. The more the hat emptied itself, the more it was full; and the emerging objects (which now included the house in Lowndes Square and a perfect dream of a place in Hampshire) grew constantly larger, and the conjurer more impressive and persuasive, and the audience more enthusiastic in its applause. At last, with a unique flourish, and a new turning-up of sleeves to prove that there was no deception, had come out of the hat the C.M.I.C., a sort of incredibly enormous Union Jack, which enwrapped all the other objects in its splendid folds. The shares of the C.M.I.C. were affectionately known in the Kaffir circus as "Solids"; they yielded handsome though irregular dividends, earned chiefly by flotation and speculation; the circus believed in them. And in view of the annual meeting of shareholders to be held on the following Tuesday afternoon (the conjurer in the chair and his hat on the table), the market price, after a period of depression, had stiffened.

Mr. Bowring's meditations were soon interrupted by a telegram. He opened it and read: "*Cook drunk again. Will dine with you Devonshire, seven-thirty. Impossible here. Have arranged about luggage.—Marie.*" Marie was Mr. Bowring's wife. He told himself that he felt greatly relieved by that telegram; he clutched at it; and his spirits seemed to rise. At any rate, since he would not now go near Lowndes Square, he could certainly laugh at the threatened robbery. He thought what a wonderful thing Providence was, after all.

"Just look at that," he said to his clerk, showing the telegram with a humorous affectation of dismay.

"Tut, tut," said the clerk, discreetly sympathetic towards his employer thug victimised by debauched cooks. "I suppose you're going down to Hampshire to-night as usual, sir?"

Mr. Bowring replied that he was, and that everything appeared to be in order for the meeting, and that he should be back on Monday afternoon or at the latest very early on Tuesday.

Then, with a few parting instructions, and with that eagle glance round his own room and into circumjacent rooms which a truly efficient head of affairs never omits on leaving business for the week-end, Mr. Bowring sedately, yet magnificently, departed from the noble registered offices of the C.M.I.C.

"Why didn't Marie telephone instead of wiring?" he mused, as his pair of greys whirled him and his coachman and his footman off to the Devonshire.

II

The Devonshire Mansion, a bright edifice of eleven storeys in
the Foster and Dicksee style, constructional ironwork by Homan,
lifts by Waygood, decorations by Waring, and terra-cotta by the
rood, is situate on the edge of Hyde Park. It is a composite building. Its foundations are firmly fixed in the Tube railway; above that
comes the wine cellarage, then the vast laundry, and then (a row
of windows scarcely level with the street) a sporting club, a billiard-room, a grill-room, and a cigarette-merchant whose name
ends in "opoulos." On the first floor is the renowned Devonshire
Mansion Restaurant. Always, in London, there is just one restaurant where, if you are an entirely correct person, "you can get a
decent meal." The place changes from season to season, but there
is never more than one of it at a time. That season it happened to
be the Devonshire. (The *chef* of the Devonshire had invented tripe
suppers, *tripes à la mode de Caen*, and these suppers—seven-and-
six—had been the rage.) Consequently all entirely correct people
fed as a matter of course at the Devonshire, since there was no
other place fit to go to. The vogue of the restaurant favourably affected the vogue of the nine floors of furnished suites above the
restaurant; they were always full; and the heavenward attics, where
the servants took off their smart liveries and became human, held
much wealth. The vogue of the restaurant also exercised a beneficial
influence over the status of the Kitcat Club, which was a cock-and-
hen club of the latest pattern and had its "house" on the third floor.

It was a little after half-past seven when Mr. Bruce Bowring
haughtily ascended the grand staircase of this resort of opulence,
and paused for an instant near the immense fireplace at the summit (September was inclement, and a fire burned nicely) to inquire
from the head-waiter whether Mrs. Bowring had secured a table.
But Marie had not arrived—Marie, who was never late! Uneasy and
chagrined, he proceeded, under the escort of the head-waiter, to
the glittering Salle Louis Quatorze and selected, because of his
morning attire, a table half-hidden behind an onyx pillar. The great
room was moderately full of fair women and possessive men, despite the month. Immediately afterwards a youngish couple (the

man handsomer and better dressed than the woman) took the table on the other side of the pillar. Mr. Bowring waited five minutes, then he ordered Sole Mornay and a bottle of Romanee-Conti, and then he waited another five minutes. He went somewhat in fear of his wife, and did not care to begin without her.

"Can't you read?" It was the youngish man at the next table speaking in a raised voice to a squinting lackey with a telegraph form in his hand. "'Solids! Solids,' my friend. 'Sell—Solids—to—any—amount—to-morrow—and—Monday.' Got it? Well, send it off at once."

"Quite clear, my lord," said the lackey, and fled. The youngish man gazed fixedly but absently at Mr. Bowring and seemed to see through him to the tapestry behind. Mr. Bowring, to his own keen annoyance, reddened. Partly to conceal the blush, and partly because it was a quarter to eight and there was the train to catch, he lowered his face, and began upon the sole. A few minutes later the lackey returned, gave some change to the youngish man, and surprised Mr. Bowring by advancing towards him and handing him an envelope—an envelope which bore on its flap the legend "Kitcat Club." The note within was scribbled in pencil in his wife's handwriting, and ran: "*Just arrived. Delayed by luggage. I'm too nervous to face the restaurant, and am eating a chop here alone. The place is fortunately empty. Come and fetch me as soon as you're ready.*"

Mr. Bowring sighed angrily. He hated his wife's club, and this succession of messages telephonic, telegraphic, and calligraphic was exasperating him.

"No answer!" he ejaculated, and then he beckoned the lackey closer. "Who's that gentleman at the next table with the lady?" he murmured.

"I'm not rightly sure, sir," was the whispered reply. "Some authorities say he's the strong man at the Hippodrome, while others affirm he's a sort of American millionaire."

"But you addressed him as 'my lord.'"

"Just then I thought he was the strong man, sir," said the lackey, retiring.

"My bill!" Mr. Bowring demanded fiercely of the waiter, and at the same time the youngish gentleman and his companion rose and departed.

At the lift Mr. Bowring found the squinting lackey in charge.

"You're the liftman, too?"

"To-night, sir, I am many things. The fact is, the regular liftman has got a couple of hours off—being the recent father of twins."

"Well—Kitcat Club."

The lift seemed to shoot far upwards, and Mr. Bowring thought the lackey had mistaken the floor, but on gaining the corridor he saw across the portals in front of him the remembered gold sign, "Kitcat Club. Members only." He pushed the door open and went in.

III

Instead of the familiar vestibule of his wife's club, Mr. Bowring discovered a small antechamber, and beyond, through a doorway half-screened by a *portière* he had glimpses of a rich, rose-lit drawing-room. In the doorway, with one hand raised to the *portière*, stood the youngish man who had forced him to blush in the restaurant.

"I beg your pardon," said Mr. Bowring, stiffly— "is this the Kitcat Club?"

The other man advanced to the outer door, his brilliant eyes fixed on Mr. Bowring's; his arm crept round the cheek of the door and came back bearing the gold sign; then he shut the door and locked it. "No, this isn't the Kitcat Club at all," he replied. "It is my flat. Come and sit down. I was expecting you."

"I shall do nothing of the kind," said Mr. Bowring disdainfully.

"But when I tell you that I know you are going to decamp to-night, Mr. Bowring—"

The youngish man smiled affably.

"Decamp?" The spine of the financier suddenly grew flaccid.

"I used the word."

"Who the devil are you?" snapped the financier, forcing his spine to rigidity.

"I am the 'friend' on the telephone. I specially wanted you at the Devonshire to-night, and I thought that the fear of a robbery at Lowndes Square might make your arrival here more certain. I am he who devised the story of the inebriated cook and favoured you with a telegram signed 'Marie.' I am the humorist who pretended in a loud voice to send off telegraphic instructions to sell 'Solids,' in order to watch your demeanour under the test. I am the expert who forged your wife's handwriting in a note from the Kitcat. I am the patron of the cross-eyed menial who gave you the note and who afterwards raised you too high in the lift. I am the artificer of this gold sign, an exact duplicate of the genuine one two floors below, which induced you to visit me. The sign alone cost me nine-and-six; the servant's livery came to two pounds fifteen. But I never consider expense when, by dint of a generous outlay, I can avoid violence. I hate violence." He gently waved the sign to and fro.

"Then my wife—" Mr. Bowring stammered in a panic rage.

"Is probably at Lowndes Square, wondering what on earth has happened to you."

Mr. Bowring took breath, remembered that he was a great man, and steadied himself.

"You must be mad," he remarked quietly. "Open this door at once."

"Perhaps," the stranger judicially admitted. "Perhaps a sort of madness. But do come and sit down. We have no time to lose."

Mr. Bowring gazed at that handsome face, with the fine nostrils, large mouth, and square, clean chin, and the dark eyes, the black hair, and long, black moustache; and he noticed the long, thin hands. "Decadent!" he decided. Nevertheless, and though it was with the air of indulging the caprice of a lunatic, he did in fact obey the stranger's request.

It was a beautiful Chippendale drawing-room that he entered. Near the hearth, to which a morsel of fire gave cheerfulness, were two easy-chairs, and between them a small table. Behind was extended a fourfold draught-screen.

"I can give you just five minutes," said Mr. Bowring, magisterially sitting down.

"They will suffice," the stranger responded, sitting down also. "You have in your pocket, Mr. Bowring—probably your breast-pocket—fifty Bank of England notes for a thousand pounds each, and a number of smaller notes amounting to another ten thousand."

"Well?"

"I must demand from you the first-named fifty."

Mr. Bowring, in the silence of the rose-lit drawing-room, thought of all the Devonshire Mansion, with its endless corridors and innumerable rooms, its acres of carpets, its forests of furniture, its gold and silver, and its jewels and its wines, its pretty women and possessive men—the whole humming microcosm founded on a unanimous pretence that the sacredness of property was a natural law. And he thought how disconcerting it was that he should be trapped there, helpless, in the very middle of the vast pretence, and forced to admit that the sacredness of property was a purely artificial convention.

"By what right do you make this demand?" he inquired, bravely sarcastic.

"By the right of my unique knowledge," said the stranger, with a bright smile. "Listen to what you and I alone know. You are at the end of the tether. The Consolidated is at the same spot. You have a past consisting chiefly of nineteen fraudulent flotations. You have paid dividends out of capital till there is no capital left. You have speculated and lost. You have cooked balance-sheets to a turn and ruined the eyesight of auditors with dust. You have lived like ten lords. Your houses are mortgaged. You own an unrivalled collection of unreceipted bills. You are worse than a common thief. (Excuse these personalities.)"

"My dear, good sir—" Mr. Bowring interrupted, grandly.

"Permit me. What is more serious, your self-confidence has been gradually deserting you. At last, perceiving that some blundering person was bound soon to put his foot through the brittle shell of your ostentation and tread on nothing, and foreseeing for yourself an immediate future consisting chiefly of Holloway, you have by a supreme effort of your genius, borrowed £60,000 from a bank on C.M.I.C. scrip, for a week (eh?), and you have arranged, you and your wife, to—melt into thin air. You will affect to set out as usual for your country place in Hampshire, but it is Southampton that will see you to-night, and Havre will see you to-morrow. You may run over to Paris to change some notes, but by Monday you will be on your way to—frankly, I don't know where; perhaps Monte Video. Of course you take the risk of extradition, but the risk is preferable to the certainty that awaits you in England. I think you will elude extradition. If I thought otherwise, I should not have had you here to-night, because, once extradited, you might begin to amuse yourself by talking about me."

"So it's blackmail," said Mr. Bowring, grim.

The dark eyes opposite to him sparkled gaily.

"It desolates me," the youngish man observed, "to have to commit you to the deep with only ten thousand. But, really, not less than fifty thousand will requite me for the brain-tissue which I have expended in the study of your interesting situation."

Mr. Bowring consulted his watch.

"Come, now," he said, huskily; "I'll give you ten thousand. I flatter myself I can look facts in the face, and so I'll give you ten thousand."

"My friend," answered the spider, "you are a judge of character. Do you honestly think I don't mean precisely what I say—to sixpence? It is eight-thirty. You are, if I may be allowed the remark, running it rather fine."

"And suppose I refuse to part?" said Mr. Bowring, after reflection. "What then?"

"I have confessed to you that I hate violence. You would therefore leave this room unmolested, but you wouldn't step off the island."

Mr. Bowring scanned the agreeable features of the stranger. Then, while the lifts were ascending and descending, and the wine was sparkling, and the jewels flashing, and the gold chinking, and the pretty women being pretty, in all the four quarters of the

Devonshire, Mr. Bruce Bowring in the silent parlour counted out fifty notes on to the table. After all, it was a fortune, that little pile of white on the crimson polished wood.

"*Bon voyage!*" said the stranger. "Don't imagine that I am not full of sympathy for you. I am. You have only been unfortunate. *Bon voyage!*"

"No! By Heaven!" Mr. Bowring almost shouted, rushing back from the door, and drawing a revolver from his hip pocket. "It's too much! I didn't mean to—but confound it! what's a revolver for?"

The youngish man jumped up quickly and put his hands on the notes.

"Violence is always foolish, Mr. Bowring," he murmured.

"Will you give them up, or won't you?"

"I won't."

The stranger's fine eyes seemed to glint with joy in the drama. "Then—"

The revolver was raised, but in the same instant a tiny hand snatched it from the hand of Mr. Bowring, who turned and beheld by his side a woman. The huge screen sank slowly and noiselessly to the floor in the surprising manner peculiar to screens that have been overset.

Mr. Bowring cursed. "An accomplice! I might have guessed!" he grumbled in final disgust.

He ran to the door, unlocked it, and was no more seen.

IV

The lady was aged twenty-seven or so; of medium height, and slim, with a plain, very intelligent and expressive face, lighted by courageous, grey eyes and crowned with loose, abundant, fluffy hair. Perhaps it was the fluffy hair, perhaps it was the mouth that twitched as she dropped the revolver—who can say?—but the whole atmosphere of the rose-lit chamber was suddenly changed. The incalculable had invaded it.

"You seem surprised, Miss Fincastle," said the possessor of the bank-notes, laughing gaily.

"Surprised!" echoed the lady, controlling that mouth. "My dear Mr. Thorold, when, strictly as a journalist, I accepted your invitation, I did not anticipate this sequel; frankly I did not."

She tried to speak coldly and evenly, on the assumption that a journalist has no sex during business hours. But just then she happened to be neither less nor more a woman than a woman always is.

"If I have had the misfortune to annoy you—!" Thorold threw up his arms in gallant despair.

"Annoy is not the word," said Miss Fincastle, nervously smiling. "May I sit down? Thanks. Let us recount. You arrive in England, from somewhere, as the son and heir of the late Ahasuerus Thorold, the New York operator, who died worth six million dollars. It becomes known that while in Algiers in the spring you stayed at the Hôtel St. James, famous as the scene of what is called the 'Algiers Mystery,' familiar to English newspaper-readers since last April. The editor of my journal therefore instructs me to obtain an interview with you. I do so. The first thing I discover is that, though an American, you have no American accent. You explain this by saying that since infancy you have always lived in Europe with your mother."

"But surely you do not doubt that I am Cecil Thorold!" said the man. Their faces were approximate over the table.

"Of course not. I merely recount. To continue. I interview you as to the Algerian mystery, and get some new items concerning it. Then you regale me with tea and your opinions, and my questions grow more personal. So it comes about that, strictly on behalf of my paper, I inquire what your recreations are. And suddenly you answer: 'Ah! My recreations! Come to dinner to-night, quite informally, and I will show you how I amuse myself!' I come. I dine. I am stuck behind that screen and told to listen. And—and—the millionaire proves to be nothing but a blackmailer."

"You must understand, my dear lady—"

"I understand everything, Mr. Thorold, except your object in admitting me to the scene."

"A whim!" cried Thorold vivaciously, "a freak of mine! Possibly due to the eternal and universal desire of man to show off before woman!"

The journalist tried to smile, but something in her face caused Thorold to run to a chiffonier.

"Drink this," he said, returning with a glass.

"I need nothing." The voice was a whisper.

"Oblige me."

Miss Fincastle drank and coughed.

"Why did you do it?" she asked sadly, looking at the notes.

"You don't mean to say," Thorold burst out, "that you are feeling sorry for Mr. Bruce Bowring? He has merely parted with what he stole. And the people from whom he stole, stole. All the activities which centre about the Stock Exchange are simply various manifestations of one primeval instinct. Suppose I had not—had not interfered. No one would have been a penny the better off except Mr. Bruce Bowring. Whereas—"

"You intend to restore this money to the Consolidated?" said Miss Fincastle eagerly.

"Not quite! The Consolidated doesn't deserve it. You must not regard its shareholders as a set of innocent shorn lambs. They knew the game. They went in for what they could get. Besides, how could I restore the money without giving myself away? I want the money myself."

"But you are a millionaire."

"It is precisely because I am a millionaire that I want more. All millionaires are like that."

"I am sorry to find you a thief, Mr. Thorold."

"A thief! No. I am only direct, I only avoid the middleman. At dinner, Miss Fincastle, you displayed somewhat advanced views about property, marriage, and the aristocracy of brains. You said that labels were for the stupid majority, and that the wise minority examined the ideas behind the labels. You label me a thief, but examine the idea, and you will perceive that you might as well call yourself a thief. Your newspaper every day suppresses the truth about the City, and it does so in order to live. In other words, it touches the pitch, it participates in the game. To-day it has a fifty-line advertisement of a false balance-sheet of the Consolidated, at two shillings a line. That five pounds, part of the loot of a great city, will help to pay for your account of our interview this after-noon."

"Our interview to-night," Miss Fincastle corrected him stiffly, "and all that I have seen and heard."

At these words she stood up, and as Cecil Thorold gazed at her his face changed.

"I shall begin to wish," he said slowly, "that I had deprived myself of the pleasure of your company this evening."

"You might have been a dead man had you done so," Miss Fincastle retorted, and observing his blank countenance she touched the revolver. "Have you forgotten already?" she asked tartly.

"Of course it wasn't loaded," he remarked. "Of course I had seen to that earlier in the day. I am not such a bungler—"

"Then I didn't save your life?"

"You force me to say that you did not, and to remind you that you gave me your word not to emerge from behind the screen. However, seeing the motive, I can only thank you for that lapse. The pity is that it hopelessly compromises you."

"Me?" exclaimed Miss Fincastle.

"You. Can't you see that you are in it, in this robbery, to give the thing a label. You were alone with the robber. You succoured the robber at a critical moment . . . 'Accomplice,' Mr. Bowring him-self said. My dear journalist, the episode of the revolver, empty though the revolver was, seals your lips."

Miss Fincastle laughed rather hysterically, leaning over the table with her hands on it.

"My dear millionaire," she said rapidly, "you don't know the new journalism, to which I have the honour to belong. You would know it better had you lived more in New York. All I have to an-nounce is that, compromised or not, a full account of this affair will appear in my paper to-morrow morning. No, I shall not in-form the police. I am a journalist simply, but a journalist I *am*."

"And your promise, which you gave me before going behind the screen, your solemn promise that you would reveal nothing? I was loth to mention it."

"Some promises, Mr. Thorold, it is a duty to break, and it is my duty to break this one. I should never have given it had I had the slightest idea of the nature of your recreations."

Thorold still smiled, though faintly.

"Really, you know," he murmured, "this is getting just a little serious."

"It is very serious," she stammered.

And then Thorold noticed that the new journalist was softly weeping.

V

The door opened.

"Miss Kitty Sartorius," said the erstwhile liftman, who was now in plain clothes and had mysteriously ceased to squint.

A beautiful girl, a girl who had remarkable loveliness and was aware of it (one of the prettiest women of the Devonshire), ran impulsively into the room and caught Miss Fincastle by the hand.

"My dearest Eve, you're crying. What's the matter?"

"Lecky," said Thorold aside to the servant. "I told you to admit no one."

The beautiful blonde turned sharply to Thorold.

"I told him I wished to enter," she said imperiously, half closing her eyes.

"Yes, sir," said Lecky. "That was it. The lady wished to enter."

Thorold bowed.

"It was sufficient," he said. "That will do, Lecky."

"Yes, sir."

"But I say, Lecky, when next you address me publicly, try to remember that I am not in the peerage."

The servant squinted.

"Certainly, sir." And he retired.

"Now we are alone," said Miss Sartorius. "Introduce us, Eve, and explain."

Miss Fincastle, having regained self-control, introduced her dear friend the radiant star of the Regency Theatre, and her acquaintance the millionaire.

"Eve didn't feel *quite* sure of you," the actress stated; "and so we arranged that if she wasn't up at my flat by nine o'clock, I was to come down and reconnoitre. What have you been doing to make Eve cry?"

"Unintentional, I assure you—" Thorold began.

"There's something between you two," said Kitty Sartorius sagaciously, in significant accents. "What is it?"

She sat down, touched her picture hat, smoothed her white gown, and tapped her foot. "What is it, now? Mr. Thorold, I think *you* had better tell me."

Thorold raised his eyebrows and obediently commenced the narration, standing with his back to the fire.

"How perfectly splendid!" Kitty exclaimed. "I'm so glad you cornered Mr. Bowring. I met him one night and I thought he was horrid. And these are the notes? Well, of all the—!"

Thorold proceeded with his story.

"Oh, but you can't do *that*, Eve!" said Kitty, suddenly serious. "You can't go and split! It would mean all sorts of bother; your wretched newspaper would be sure to keep you hanging about in London, and we shouldn't be able to start on our holiday to-morrow. Eve and I are starting on quite a long tour to-morrow, Mr. Thorold; we begin with Ostend."

"Indeed!" said Thorold. "I, too, am going in that direction soon. Perhaps we may meet."

"I hope so," Kitty smiled, and then she looked at Eve Fincastle. "You really mustn't do that, Eve," she said.

"I must, I must!" Miss Fincastle insisted, clenching her hands.

"And she will," said Kitty tragically, after considering her friend's face. "She will, and our holiday's ruined. I see it—I see it plainly. She's in one of her stupid conscientious moods. She's fearfully advanced and careless and unconventional in theory, Eve is;

but when it comes to practice! Mr. Thorold, you have just got everything into a dreadful knot. Why did you want those notes so very particularly?"

"I don't want them so very particularly."

"Well, anyhow, it's a most peculiar predicament. Mr. Bowring doesn't count, and this Consolidated thingummy isn't any the worse off. Nobody suffers who oughtn't to suffer. It's your unlawful gain that's wrong. Why not pitch the wretched notes in the fire?" Kitty laughed at her own playful humour.

"Certainly," said Thorold. And with a quick movement he put the fifty trifles in the grate, where they made a bluish yellow flame.

Both the women screamed and sprang up.

"*Mr.* Thorold!"

"Mr. *Thorold!*" ("He's adorable!" Kitty breathed.)

"The incident, I venture to hope, is now closed," said Thorold calmly, but with his dark eyes sparkling. "I must thank you both for a very enjoyable evening. Some day, perhaps, I may have an opportunity of further explaining my philosophy to you."

A Comedy on the Gold Coast

I

It was five o'clock on an afternoon in mid-September, and a couple of American millionaires (they abounded that year, did millionaires) sat chatting together on the wide terrace which separates the entrance to the Kursaal from the promenade. Some yards away, against the balustrade of the terrace, in the natural, unconsidered attitude of one to whom short frocks are a matter of history, certainly, but very recent history, stood a charming and imperious girl; you could see that she was eating chocolate while meditating upon the riddle of life. The elder millionaire glanced at every pretty woman within view, excepting only the girl; but his companion seemed to be intent on counting the chocolates.

The immense crystal dome of the Kursaal dominated the gold coast, and on either side of the great building were stretched out in a straight line the hotels, the restaurants, the *cafés*, the shops, the theatres, the concert-halls, and the pawnbrokers of the City of Pleasure—Ostend. At one extremity of that long array of ornate white architecture (which resembled the icing on a bride-cake more than the roofs of men) was the palace of a king; at the other were the lighthouse and the railway-signals which guided into the city the continuously arriving cargoes of wealth, beauty, and desire. In front, the ocean, grey and lethargic, idly beat up a little genteel foam under the promenade for the wetting of pink feet and stylish bathing-costumes. And after a hard day's work, the sun, by arrangement with the authorities during August and September, was setting over the sea exactly opposite the superb portals of the Kursaal.

The younger of the millionaires was Cecil Thorold. The other, a man fifty-five or so, was Simeon Rainshore, father of the girl at the balustrade, and president of the famous Dry Goods Trust, of exciting memory. The contrast between the two men, alike only in extreme riches, was remarkable: Cecil still youthful, slim, dark, languid of movement, with delicate features, eyes almost Spanish, and an accent of purest English; and Rainshore with his nasal twang, his stout frame, his rounded, bluish-red chin, his little eyes, and that demeanour of false briskness by means of which ageing men seek to prove to themselves that they are as young as ever they were. Simeon had been a friend and opponent of Cecil's father; in former days those twain had victimised each other for colossal sums. Consequently Simeon had been glad to meet the son of his dead antagonist, and, in less than a week of Ostend repose, despite a fundamental disparity of temperament, the formidable president and the Europeanised wanderer had achieved a sort of intimacy, an intimacy which was about to be intensified.

"The difference between you and me is this," Cecil was saying. "You exhaust yourself by making money among men who are all bent on making money, in a place specially set apart for the purpose. I amuse myself by making money among men who, having made or inherited money, are bent on spending it, in places specially set apart for the purpose. I take people off their guard. They don't precisely see me coming. I don't rent an office and put up a sign which is equivalent to announcing that the rest of the world had better look out for itself. Our codes are the same, but is not my way more original and more diverting? Look at this place. Half the wealth of Europe is collected here; the other half is at Trouville. The entire coast reeks of money; the sands are golden with it. You've only to put out your hand—so!"

"So?" ejaculated Rainshore, quizzical. "How? Show me?"

"Ah! That would be telling."

"I guess you wouldn't get much out of Simeon—not as much as your father did."

"Do you imagine I should try?" said Cecil gravely. "My amusements are always discreet."

"But you confess you are often bored. Now, on Wall Street we are never bored."

"Yes," Cecil admitted. "I embarked on these—these enterprises mainly to escape boredom."

"You ought to marry," said Rainshore pointedly. "You ought to marry, my friend."

"I have my yacht."

"No doubt. And she's a beauty, and feminine too; but not feminine enough. You ought to marry. Now, I'll—"

Mr. Rainshore paused. His daughter had suddenly ceased to eat chocolates and was leaning over the balustrade in order to converse with a tall, young man whose fair, tanned face and white hat overtopped the carved masonry and were thus visible to the millionaires. The latter glanced at one another and then glanced away, each slightly self-conscious.

"I thought Mr. Vaux-Lowry had left?" said Cecil.

"He came back last night," Rainshore replied curtly. "And he leaves again to-night."

"Then—then it's a match after all!" Cecil ventured.

"Who says that?" was Simeon's sharp inquiry.

"The birds of the air whisper it. One heard it at every corner three days ago."

Rainshore turned his chair a little towards Cecil's. "You'll allow I ought to know something about it," he said. "Well, I tell you it's a lie."

"I'm sorry I mentioned it," Cecil apologised.

"Not at all," said Simeon, stroking his chin. "I'm glad you did. Because now you can just tell all the birds of the air direct from me that in this particular case there isn't going to be the usual alliance between the beauty and dollars of America and the aristocratic blood of Great Britain. Listen right here," he continued confidentially, like a man whose secret feelings have been inconveniencing him for several hours. "This young spark—mind, I've nothing against him!—asks me to consent to his engagement with

Geraldine. I tell him that I intend to settle half a million dollars on my daughter, and that the man she marries must cover that half-million with another. He says he has a thousand a year of his own, pounds—just nice for Geraldine's gloves and candy!—and that he is the heir of his uncle, Lord Lowry; and that there is an entail; and that Lord Lowry is very rich, very old, and very unmarried; but that, being also very peculiar, he won't come down with any money. It occurs to me to remark: 'Suppose Lord Lowry marries and develops into the father of a man-child, where do *you* come in, Mr. Vaux-Lowry?' 'Oho! Lord Lowry marry! Impossible! Laughable!' Then Geraldine begins to worry at me, and her mother too. And so I kind of issue an ultimatum—namely, I will consent to an engagement without a settlement if, on the marriage, Lord Lowry will give a note of hand for half a million dollars to Geraldine, payable on *his* marriage. See? My lord's nephew goes off to persuade my lord, and returns with my lord's answer in an envelope sealed with the great seal. I open it and I read—this is what I read: 'To Mr. S. Rainshore, American draper. Sir—As a humorist you rank high. Accept the admiration of Your obedient servant, Lowry.'"

The millionaire laughed.

"Oh! It's clever enough!" said Rainshore. "It's very English and grand. Dashed if I don't admire it! All the same, I've requested Mr. Vaux-Lowry, under the circumstances, to quit this town. I didn't show him the letter—no. I spared his delicate feelings. I merely told him Lord Lowry had refused, and that I would be ready to consider his application favourably any time when he happened to have half a million dollars in his pocket."

"And Miss Geraldine?"

"She's flying the red flag, but she knows when my back's against the wall. She knows her father. She'll recover. Great Scott! She's eighteen, he's twenty-one; the whole affair is a high farce. And, moreover, I guess I want Geraldine to marry an American, after all."

"And if she elopes?" Cecil murmured as if to himself, gazing at the set features of the girl, who was now alone once more.

"*Elopes?*"

Rainshore's face reddened as his mood shifted suddenly from indulgent cynicism to profound anger. Cecil was amazed at the transformation, until he remembered to have heard long ago that Simeon himself had eloped.

"It was just a fancy that flashed into my mind," Cecil smiled diplomatically.

"I should let it flash out again if I were you," said Rainshore, with a certain grimness. And Cecil perceived the truth of the maxim that a parent can never forgive his own fault in his child.

II

"You've come to sympathise with me," said Geraldine Rainshore calmly, as Cecil, leaving the father for a few moments, strolled across the terrace towards the daughter.

"It's my honest, kindly face that gives me away," he responded lightly. "But what am I to sympathise with you about?"

"You know what," the girl said briefly.

They stood together near the balustrade, looking out over the sea into the crimson eye of the sun; and all the afternoon activities of Ostend were surging round them—the muffled sound of musical instruments from within the Kursaal, the shrill cries of late bathers from the shore, the toot of a tramway-horn to the left, the roar of a siren to the right, and everywhere the ceaseless hum of an existence at once gay, feverish, and futile; but Cecil was conscious of nothing but the individuality by his side. Some women, he reflected, are older at eighteen than they are at thirty-eight, and Geraldine was one of those. She happened to be very young and very old at the same time. She might be immature, crude, even gawky in her girlishness; but she was just then in the first flush of mentally realising the absolute independence of the human spirit. She had force, and she had also the enterprise to act on it.

As Cecil glanced at her intelligent, expressive face, he thought of her playing with life as a child plays with a razor.

"You mean—?" he inquired.

"I mean that father has been talking about me to you. I could tell by his eyes. Well?"

"Your directness unnerves me," he smiled.

"Pull yourself together, then, Mr. Thorold. Be a man."

"Will you let me treat you as a friend?"

"Why, yes," she said, "if you'll promise not to tell me I'm only eighteen."

"I am incapable of such rudeness," Cecil replied. "A woman is as old as she feels. You feel at least thirty; therefore you are at least thirty. This being understood, I am going to suggest, as a friend, that if you and Mr. Vaux-Lowry are—perhaps pardonably—contemplating any extreme step—"

"Extreme step, Mr. Thorold?"

"Anything rash."

"And suppose we are?" Geraldine demanded, raising her chin scornfully and defiantly and dangling her parasol.

"I should respectfully and confidentially advise you to refrain. Be content to wait, my dear middle-aged woman. Your father may relent. And also, I have a notion that I may be able to—to—"

"Help us?"

"Possibly."

"You are real good," said Geraldine coldly. "But what gave you the idea that Harry and I were meaning to—?"

"Something in your eyes—your fine, daring eyes. I read you as you read your father, you see?"

"Well, then, Mr. Thorold, there's something wrong with my fine, daring eyes. I'm just the last girl in all America to do anything—rash. Why! if I did anything rash, I'm sure I should feel ever afterwards as if I wanted to be excused off the very face of the earth. I'm that sort of girl. Do you think I don't know that father will give way? I guess he's just got to. With time and hammering, you can knock sense into the head of any parent."

"I apologise," said Cecil, both startled and convinced. "And I congratulate Mr. Vaux-Lowry."

"Say. You like Harry, don't you?"

"Very much. He's the ideal type of Englishman."

Geraldine nodded sweetly. "And so obedient! He does everything I tell him. He is leaving for England to-night, not because father asked him to, but because I did. I'm going to take mother to Brussels for a few days' shopping—lace, you know. That will give father an opportunity to meditate in solitude on his own greatness. Tell me, Mr. Thorold, do you consider that Harry and I would be justified in corresponding secretly?"

Cecil assumed a pose of judicial gravity.

"I think you would," he decided. "But don't tell anyone I said so."

"Not even Harry?"

She ran off into the Kursaal, saying she must seek her mother. But instead of seeking her mother, Geraldine passed straight through the concert-hall, where a thousand and one wondrously attired women were doing fancy needle-work to the accompaniment of a band of music, into the maze of corridors beyond, and so to the rear entrance of the Kursaal on the Boulevard van Isoghem. Here she met Mr. Harry Vaux-Lowry, who was most obviously waiting for her. They crossed the road to the empty tramway waiting-room and entered it and sat down; and by the mere act of looking into each other's eyes, these two—the stiff, simple, honest-faced young Englishman with "Oxford" written all over him, and the charming child of a civilisation equally proud, but with fewer conventions, suddenly transformed the little bureau into a Cupid's bower.

"It's just as I thought, you darling boy," Geraldine began to talk rapidly. "Father's the least bit in the world scared; and when he's scared, he's bound to confide in someone; and he's confided in that sweet Mr. Thorold. And Mr. Thorold has been requested to reason with me and advise me to be a good girl and wait. I know what *that* means. It means that father thinks we shall soon forget each other, my poor Harry. And I do believe it means that father wants me to marry Mr. Thorold."

"What did you say to him, dear?" the lover demanded, pale.

"Trust me to fool him, Harry. I simply walked round him. He thinks we are going to be very good and wait patiently. As if father ever *would* give way until he was forced!"

She laughed disdainfully. "So we're perfectly safe so long as we act with discretion. Now let's clearly understand. To-day's Monday. You return to England to-night."

"Yes. And I'll arrange about the licence and things."

"Your cousin Mary is just as important as the licence, Harry," said Geraldine primly.

"She will come. You may rely on her being at Ostend with me on Thursday.

"Very well. In the meantime, I behave as if life were a blank. Brussels will put them off the scent. Mother and I will return from there on Thursday afternoon. That night there is a *soirée dansante* at the Kursaal. Mother will say she is too tired to go to it, but she will have to go all the same. I will dance before all men till a quarter to ten—I will even dance with Mr. Thorold. What a pity I can't dance before father, but he's certain to be in the gambling-rooms then, winning money; he always is at that hour! At a quarter to ten I will slip out, and you'll be here at this back door with a carriage. We drive to the quay and just catch the 11.5 steamer, and I meet your cousin Mary. On Friday morning we are married; and then, then we shall be in a position to talk to father. He'll pretend to be furious, but he can't say much, because he eloped himself. Didn't you know?"

"I didn't," said Harry, with a certain dryness.

"Oh, yes! It's in the family! But you needn't look so starched, my English lord." He took her hand. "You're sure your uncle won't disinherit you, or anything horrid of that kind?"

"He can't," said Harry.

"What a perfectly lovely country England is!" Geraldine exclaimed. "Fancy the poor old thing not being *able* to disinherit you! Why, it's just too delicious for words!"

And for some reason or other he kissed her violently.

Then an official entered the bureau and asked them if they wanted to go to Blankenburghe; because, if so, the tram was awaiting their distinguished pleasure. They looked at each other foolishly and sidled out, and the bureau ceased to be Cupid's bower.

III

By Simeon's request, Cecil dined with the Rainshores that night at the Continental. After dinner they all sat out on the balcony and sustained themselves with coffee while watching the gay traffic of the Digue, the brilliant illumination of the Kursaal, and the distant lights on the invisible but murmuring sea. Geraldine was in one of her moods of philosophic pessimism, and would persist in dwelling on the uncertainty of riches and the vicissitudes of millionaires. She found a text in the famous Bowring case, of which the newspaper contained many interesting details.

"I wonder if he'll be caught?" she remarked.

"I wonder," said Cecil.

"What do you think, father?"

"I think you had better go to bed," Simeon replied.

The chit rose and kissed him duteously.

"Good night," she said. "Aren't you glad the sea keeps so calm?"

"Why?"

"Can you ask? Mr. Vaux-Lowry crosses to-night, and he's a dreadfully bad sailor. Come along, mother. Mr. Thorold, when mother and I return from Brussels, we shall expect to be taken for a cruise in the *Claribel*."

Simeon sighed with relief upon the departure of his family and began a fresh cigar. On the whole, his day had been rather too domestic. He was quite pleased when Cecil, having apparently by accident broached the subject of the Dry Goods Trust, proceeded to exhibit a minute curiosity concerning the past, the present, and the future of the greatest of all the Rainshore enterprises.

"Are you thinking of coming in?" Simeon demanded at length, pricking up his ears.

"No," said Cecil, "I'm thinking of going out. The fact is, I haven't mentioned it before, but I'm ready to sell a very large block of shares."

"The deuce you are!" Simeon exclaimed. "And what do you call a very large block?"

"Well," said Cecil, "it would cost me nearly half a million to take them up now."

"Dollars?"

"Pounds sterling. Twenty-five thousand shares, at 95 3/8."

Rainshore whistled two bars of "Follow me!" from "The Belle of New York."

"Is this how you amuse yourself at Ostend?" he inquired.

Cecil smiled: "This is quite an exceptional transaction. And not too profitable, either."

"But you can't dump that lot on the market," Simeon protested.

"Yes, I can," said Cecil. "I must, and I will. There are reasons. You yourself wouldn't care to handle it, I suppose?"

The president of the Trust pondered.

"I'd handle it at 93 3/8," he answered quietly.

"Oh, come! That's dropping two points!" said Cecil, shocked. "A minute ago you were prophesying a further rise."

Rainshore's face gleamed out momentarily in the darkness as he puffed at his cigar.

"If you must unload," he remarked, as if addressing the red end of the cigar, "I'm your man at 93 3/8."

Cecil argued: but Simeon Rainshore never argued—it was not his method. In a quarter of an hour the younger man had contracted to sell twenty-five thousand shares of a hundred dollars each in the United States Dry Goods Trust at two points below the current market quotation, and six and five eighths points below par.

The hoot of an outgoing steamer sounded across the city.

"I must go," said Cecil.

"You're in a mighty hurry," Simeon complained.

IV

Five minutes later Cecil was in his own rooms at the Hotel de la Plage. Soon there was a discreet knock at the door.

"Come in, Lecky," he said.

It was his servant who entered, the small, thin man with very mobile eyes and of no particular age, who, in various capacities and incarnations—now as liftman, now as financial agent, now as no matter what—assisted Cecil in his diversions.

"Mr. Vaux-Lowry really did go by the boat, Sir."

"Good. And you have given directions about the yacht?"

"The affair is in order."

"And you've procured one of Mr. Rainshore's Homburg hats?"

"It is in your dressing-room. There was no mark of identification on it. So, in order to smooth the difficulties of the police when they find it on the beach, I have taken the liberty of writing Mr. Rainshore's name on the lining."

"A kindly thought," said Cecil. "You'll catch the special G.S.N. steamer direct for London at 1 a.m. That will get you into town before two o'clock to-morrow afternoon. Things have turned out as I expected, and I've nothing else to say to you; but, before leaving me, perhaps you had better repeat your instructions."

"With pleasure, sir," said Lecky. "Tuesday afternoon.—I call at Cloak Lane and intimate that we want to sell Dry Goods shares. I ineffectually try to conceal a secret cause for alarm, and I gradually disclose the fact that we are very anxious indeed to sell really a lot of Dry Goods shares, in a hurry. I permit myself to be pumped, and the information is wormed out of me that Mr. Simeon Rainshore has disappeared, has possibly committed suicide; but that, at present, no one is aware of this except ourselves. I express doubts as to the soundness of the Trust, and I remark on the unfortunateness of this disappearance so soon after the lamentable panic connected with the lately vanished Bruce Bowring and his companies. I send our friends on 'change with orders to see what they can do and to report. I then go to Birchin Lane and repeat the performance there without variation. Then I call at the City office of the *Evening Messenger* and talk privily in a despondent vein with the financial editor concerning the Trust, but I breathe not a word as to Mr. Rainshore's disappearance. Wednesday morning.— The rot in Dry Goods has set in sharply, but I am now, very foolishly, disposed to haggle about the selling price. Our friends urge me to accept what I can get, and I leave them, saying that I must telegraph to you. Wednesday afternoon.—I see a reporter of the *Morning Journal* and let out that Simeon Rainshore has disappeared. The *Journal* will wire to Ostend for confirmation, which confirmation it will receive. Thursday morning.—The bottom is knocked out of the price of Dry Goods shares. Then I am to call on our other friends in Throgmorton Street and tell them to buy, buy, buy, in London, New York, Paris, everywhere."

"Go in peace," said Cecil. "If we are lucky, the price will drop to seventy."

V

"I see, Mr. Thorold," said Geraldine Rainshore, "that you are about to ask me for the next dance. It is yours."

"You are the queen of diviners," Cecil replied, bowing.

It was precisely half-past nine on Thursday evening, and they had met in a corner of the pillared and balconied *salle de danse*, in the Kursaal behind the concert-hall. The slippery, glittering floor was crowded with dancers—the men in ordinary evening dress, the women very variously attired, save that nearly all wore picture-hats. Geraldine was in a white frock, high at the neck, with a large hat of black velvet; and amidst that brilliant, multicoloured, light-hearted throng, lit by the blaze of the electric chandeliers and swayed by the irresistible melody of the "Doctrinen" waltz, the young girl, simply dressed as she was, easily held her own.

"So you've come back from Brussels?" Cecil said, taking her arm and waist.

"Yes. We arrived just on time for dinner. But what have you been doing with father? We've seen nothing of him."

"Ah!" said Cecil mysteriously. "We've been on a little voyage, and, like you, we've only just returned."

"In the *Claribel?*"

He nodded.

"You might have waited," she pouted.

"Perhaps you wouldn't have liked it. Things happened, you know."

"Why, what? Do tell me."

"Well, you left your poor father alone, and he was moping all day on Tuesday. So on Tuesday night I had the happy idea of going out in the yacht to witness a sham night attack by the French Channel Squadron on Calais. I caught your honoured parent just as he was retiring to bed, and we went. He was only too glad. But we hadn't left the harbour much more than an hour and a half when our engines broke down."

"What fun! And at night, too!"

"Yes. Wasn't it? The shaft was broken. So we didn't see much of any night attack on Calais. Fortunately the weather was all that the weather ought to be when a ship's engines break down. Still, it took us over forty hours to repair—over forty hours! I'm proud we were able to do the thing without being ignominiously towed into port. But I fear your father may have grown a little impatient, though we had excellent views of Ostend and Dunkirk, and the passing vessels were a constant diversion."

"Was there plenty to eat?" Geraldine asked simply.

"Ample."

"Then father wouldn't really mind. When did you land?"

"About an hour ago. Your father did not expect you to-night, I fancy. He dressed and went straight to the tables. He has to make up for a night lost, you see."

They danced in silence for a few moments, and then suddenly Geraldine said—

"Will you excuse me? I feel tired. Good night."

The clock under the orchestra showed seventeen minutes to ten.

"Instantly?" Cecil queried.

"Instantly." And the girl added, with a hint of mischief in her voice, as she shook hands: "I look on you as quite a friend since our last little talk; so you will excuse this abruptness, won't you?"

He was about to answer when a sort of commotion arose ear behind them. Still holding her hand he turned to look.

"Why!" he said. "It's your mother! She must be unwell!"

Mrs. Rainshore, stout, and robed, as always, in tight, sumptuous black, sat among a little bevy of chaperons. She held a newspaper in trembling hands, and she was uttering a succession of staccato "Oh-oh's," while everyone in the vicinity gazed at her with alarm. Then she dropped the paper, and, murmuring, "Simeon's dead!" sank gently to the polished floor just as Cecil and Geraldine approached.

Geraldine's first instinctive move was to seize the newspaper, which was that day's Paris edition of the *New York Herald*. She read the headlines in a flash: "Strange disappearance of Simeon Rainshore. Suicide feared. Takes advantage of his family's absence. Heavy drop in Dry Goods. Shares at 72 and still falling."

VI

"My good Rebecca, I assure you that I am alive."

This was Mr. Rainshore's attempt to calm the hysteric sobbing of his wife, who had recovered from her short swoon in the little retreat of the person who sold Tauchnitzes, picture-postcards, and French novels, between the main corridor and the reading-rooms. Geraldine and Cecil were also in the tiny chamber.

"As for this," Simeon continued, kicking the newspaper, "it's a singular thing that a man can't take a couple of days off without upsetting the entire universe. What should you do in my place, Thorold? This is the fault of your shaft."

"I should buy Dry Goods shares," said Cecil.

"And I will."

There was an imperative knock at the door. An official of police entered.

"Monsieur Ryneshor?"

"The same."

"We have received telegraphs from New York and Londres to demand if you are dead."

"I am not. I still live."

"But Monsieur's hat has been found on the beach."

"My hat?"

"It carries Monsieur's name."

"Then it isn't mine, sir."

"*Mais comment donc—?*"

"I tell you it isn't mine, sir."

"Don't be angry, Simeon," his wife pleaded between her sobs.

The exit of the official was immediately followed by another summons for admission, even more imperative. A lady entered and handed to Simeon a card: "Miss Eve Fincastle. *The Morning Journal.*"

"My paper—" she began.

"You wish to know if I exist, madam!" said Simeon.

"I—" Miss Fincastle caught sight of Cecil Thorold, paused, and bowed stiffly. Cecil bowed; he also blushed.

"I continue to exist, madam," Simeon proceeded. "I have not killed myself. But homicide of some sort is not improbable if— In short, madam, good night!"

Miss Fincastle, with a long, searching, silent look at Cecil, departed.

"Bolt that door," said Simeon to his daughter.

Then there was a third knock, followed by a hammering.

"Go away!" Simeon commanded.

"Open the door!" pleaded a muffled voice.

"It's Harry!" Geraldine whispered solemnly in Cecil's ear. "Please go and calm him. Tell him I say it's too late to-night."

Cecil went, astounded.

"What's happened to Geraldine?" cried the boy, extremely excited, in the corridor. "There are all sorts of rumours. Is she ill?"

Cecil gave an explanation, and in his turn asked for another one. "You look unnerved," he said. "What are you doing here? What is it? Come and have a drink. And tell me all, my young friend." And when, over cognac, he had learnt the details of a scheme which had no connection with his own, he exclaimed, with the utmost sincerity: "The minx! The minx!"

"What do you mean?" inquired Harry Vaux-Lowry.

"I mean that you and the minx have had the nearest possible shave of ruining your united careers. Listen to me. Give it up, my boy. I'll try to arrange things. You delivered a letter to the father-in-law of your desire a few days ago. I'll give you another one to deliver, and I fancy the result will be, different."

The letter which Cecil wrote ran thus:—

"Dear Rainshore,—I enclose cheque for £100,000. It represents part of the gold that can be picked up on the gold coast by putting out one's hand—so! You will observe that it is dated the day after the next settling-day of the London Stock Exchange. I contracted on Monday last to sell you 25,000 shares of a certain Trust at 93 3/8, I did not possess the shares then, but my agents have to-day bought them for me at an average price of 72. I stand to realise, therefore, rather more than half a million dollars. The round half-million Mr. Vaux-Lowry happens to bring you in his pocket; you will not forget your promise to him that when he did so you would consider his application favourably. I wish to make no profit out of the little transaction, but I will venture to keep the balance for out-of-pocket expenses, such as mending the *Claribel's* shaft. (How convenient it is to have a yacht that will break down when required!) The shares will doubtless recover in due course, and I hope the reputation of the Trust may not suffer, and that for the sake of old times with my father you will regard the episode in its proper light and bear me no ill-will.—Yours sincerely, C. Thorold."

The next day the engagement of Mr. Harry Nigel Selincourt Vaux-Lowry and Miss Geraldine Rainshore was announced to two continents.

A Bracelet at Bruges

The bracelet had fallen into the canal.

And the fact that the canal was the most picturesque canal in the old Flemish city of Bruges, and that the ripples caused by the splash of the bracelet had disturbed reflections of wondrous belfries, towers, steeples, and other unique examples of Gothic architecture, did nothing whatever to assuage the sudden agony of that disappearance. For the bracelet had been given to Kitty Sartorius by her grateful and lordly manager, Lionel Belmont (U.S.A.), upon the completion of the unexampled run of "The Delmonico Doll," at the Regency Theatre, London. And its diamonds were worth five hundred pounds, to say nothing of the gold.

The beautiful Kitty, and her friend Eve Fincastle, the journalist, having exhausted Ostend, had duly arrived at Bruges in the course of their holiday tour. The question of Kitty's jewellery had arisen at the start. Kitty had insisted that she must travel with all her jewels, according to the custom of theatrical stars of great magnitude. Eve had equally insisted that Kitty must travel without jewels, and had exhorted her to remember the days of her simplicity. They compromised. Kitty was allowed to bring the bracelet, but nothing else gave the usual half-dozen rings. The ravishing creature could not have persuaded herself to leave the bracelet behind, because it was so recent a gift and still new and strange and heavenly to her. But, since prudence forbade even Kitty

41

to let the trifle lie about in hotel bedrooms, she was obliged always to wear it. And she had been wearing it this bright afternoon in early October, when the girls, during a stroll, had met one of their new friends, Madame Lawrence, on the world-famous Quai du Rosaire, just at the back of the Hotel de Ville and the Halles.

Madame Lawrence resided permanently in Bruges. She was between twenty-five and forty-five, dark, with the air of continually subduing a natural instinct to dash, and well dressed in black. Equally interested in the peerage and in the poor, she had made the acquaintance of Eve and Kitty at the Hôtel de la Grande Place, where she called from time to time to induce English travellers to buy genuine Bruges lace, wrought under her own supervision by her own paupers. She was Belgian by birth, and when complimented on her fluent and correct English, she gave all the praise to her deceased husband, an English barrister. She had settled in Bruges like many people settle there, because Bruges is inexpensive, picturesque, and inordinately respectable. Besides an English church and chaplain, it has two cathedrals and an episcopal palace, with a real bishop in it.

"What an exquisite bracelet! May I look at it?" It was these simple but ecstatic words, spoken with Madame Lawrence charming foreign accent, which had begun the tragedy. The three women had stopped to admire the always admirable view from the little quay, and they were leaning over the rails when Kitty unclasped the bracelet for the inspection of the widow. The next instant there was a *plop!* an affrighted exclamation from Madame Lawrence in her native tongue, and the bracelet was engulfed before the very eyes of all three.

The three looked at each other non-plussed. Then they looked around, but not a single person was in sight. Then, for some reason which, doubtless, psychology can explain, they stared hard at the water, though the water there was just as black and foul as it is everywhere else in the canal system of Bruges.

"Surely you've not dropped it!" Eve Fincastle exclaimed in a voice of horror. Yet she knew positively that Madame Lawrence had.

The delinquent took a handkerchief from her muff and sobbed into it. And between her sobs she murmured: "We must inform the police."

"Yes, of course," said Kitty, with the lightness of one to whom a five-hundred-pound bracelet is a bagatelle. "They'll fish it up in no time."

"Well," Eve decided, "you go to the police at once, Kitty; and Madame Lawrence will go with you, because she speaks French, and I'll stay here to mark the exact spot."

The other two started, but Madame Lawrence, after a few steps, put her hand to her side. "I can't," she sighed, pale. "I am too upset. I cannot walk. You go with Miss Sartorius," she said to Eve, "and I will stay," and she leaned heavily against the railings.

Eve and Kitty ran off, just as if it was an affair of seconds, and the bracelet had to be saved from drowning. But they had scarcely turned the corner, thirty yards away, when they reappeared in company with a high official of police, whom, by the most lucky chance in the world, they had encountered in the covered passage leading to the Place du Bourg. This official, instantly enslaved by Kitty's beauty, proved to be the very mirror of politeness and optimism. He took their names and addresses, and a full description of the bracelet, and informed them that at that place the canal was nine feet deep. He said that the bracelet should undoubtedly be recovered on the morrow, but that, as dusk was imminent, it would be futile to commence angling that night. In the meantime the loss should be kept secret; and to make all sure, a succession of gendarmes should guard the spot during the night.

Kitty grew radiant, and rewarded the gallant officer with smiles; Eve was satisfied, and the face of Madame Lawrence wore a less mournful hue.

"And now," said Kitty to Madame, when everything had been arranged, and the first of the gendarmes was duly installed at the exact spot against the railings, "you must come and take tea with us in our winter garden; and be gay! Smile: I insist. And I insist that you don't worry."

Madame Lawrence tried feebly to smile.

"You are very good-natured," she stammered.

Which was decidedly true.

II

The winter-garden of the Hôtel de la Grande Place, referred to in all the hotel's advertisements, was merely the inner court of the hotel, roofed in by glass at the height of the first storey. Cane flourished there, in the shape of lounge-chairs, but no other plant. One of the lounge chairs was occupied when, just as the carillon in the belfry at the other end of the Place began to play Gounod's "Nazareth," indicating the hour of five o'clock, the three ladies entered the winter-garden. Apparently the toilettes of two of them had been adjusted and embellished as for a somewhat ceremonious occasion.

"Lo!" cried Kitty Sartorius, when she perceived the occupant of the chair, "the millionaire! Mr. Thorold, how charming of you to reappear like this! I invite you to tea."

Cecil Thorold rose with appropriate eagerness.

"Delighted!" he said, smiling, and then explained that he had arrived from Ostend about two hours before and had taken rooms in the hotel.

"You knew we were staying here?" Eve asked as he shook hands with her.

"No," he replied; "but I am very glad to find you again."

"Are you?" She spoke languidly, but her colour heightened and those eyes of hers sparkled.

"Madame Lawrence," Kitty chirruped, "let me present Mr. Cecil Thorold. He is appallingly rich, but we mustn't let that frighten us."

From a mouth less adorable than the mouth of Miss Sartorius such an introduction might have been judged lacking in the elements of good form, but for more than two years now Kitty had known that whatever she did or said was perfectly correct because she did or said it. The new acquaintances laughed amiably and a certain intimacy was at once established.

"Shall I order tea, dear?" Eve suggested.

"No, dear," said Kitty quietly. "We will wait for the Count."

"The Count?" demanded Cecil Thorold.

"The Comte d'Avrec," Kitty explained. "He is staying here."

"A French nobleman, doubtless?"

"Yes," said Kitty; and she added, "you will like him. He is an archæologist, and a musician—oh, and lots of things!"

"If I am one minute late, I entreat pardon," said a fine tenor voice at the door.

It was the Count. After he had been introduced to Madame Lawrence, and Cecil Thorold had been introduced to him, tea was served.

Now, the Comte d'Avrec was everything that a French count ought to be. As dark as Cecil Thorold, and even handsomer, he was a little older and a little taller than the millionaire, and a short, pointed, black beard, exquisitely trimmed, gave him an appearance of staid reliability which Cecil lacked. His bow was a vertebrate poem, his smile a consolation for all misfortunes, and he managed his hat, stick, gloves, and cup with the dazzling assurance of a conjurer. To observe him at afternoon tea was to be convinced that he had been specially created to shine gloriously in drawing-rooms, winter-gardens, and *tables d'hôte*. He was one of those men who always do the right thing at the right moment, who are capable of speaking an indefinite number of languages with absolute purity of accent (he spoke English much better than Madame Lawrence), and who can and do discourse with *verve* and accuracy on all sciences, arts, sports, and religions. In short, he was a phoenix of a count; and this was certainly the opinion of Miss Kitty Sartorius and of Miss Eve Fincastle, both of whom reckoned that what they did not know about men might be ignored. Kitty and the Count, it soon became evident, were mutually attracted; their souls were approaching each other with a velocity which increased inversely as the square of the lessening distance between them. And Eve was watching this approximation with undisguised interest and relish.

Nothing of the least importance occurred, save the Count's marvellous exhibition of how to behave at afternoon tea, until the refection was nearly over; and then, during a brief pause in the talk, Cecil, who was sitting to the left of Madame Lawrence, looked sharply round at the right shoulder of his tweed coat; he repeated the gesture a second and yet a third time.

"What is the matter with the man?" asked Eve Fincastle. Both she and Kitty were extremely bright, animated, and even excited.

"Nothing. I thought I saw something on my shoulder, that's all," said Cecil. "Ah! It's only a bit of thread." And he picked off the thread with his left hand and held it before Madame Lawrence. "See! It's a piece of thin black silk, knotted. At first I took it for an insect—you know how queer things look out of the corner of your eye. Pardon!" He had dropped the fragment on to Madame Lawrence's black silk dress. "Now it's lost."

"If you will excuse me, kind friends," said Madame Lawrence, "I will go." She spoke hurriedly, and as though in mental distress.

"Poor thing!" Kitty Sartorius exclaimed when the widow had gone. "She's still dreadfully upset"; and Kitty and Eve proceeded jointly to relate the story of the diamond bracelet, upon which hitherto they had kept silence (though with difficulty), out of regard for Madame Lawrence's feelings.

Cecil made almost no comment.

The Count, with the sympathetic excitability of his race, walked up and down the winter-garden, asseverating earnestly that such clumsiness amounted to a crime; then he grew calm and confessed that he shared the optimism of the police as to the recovery of the bracelet; lastly he complimented Kitty on her equable demeanour under this affliction.

"Do you know, Count," said Cecil Thorold, later, after they had all four ascended to the drawing-room overlooking the Grande Place, "I was quite surprised when I saw at tea that you had to be introduced to Madame Lawrence."

"Why so, my dear Mr. Thorold?" the Count inquired suavely.

"I thought I had seen you together in Ostend a few days ago."

The Count shook his wonderful head.

"Perhaps you have a brother?" Cecil paused.

"No," said the Count. "But it is a favourite theory of mine that everyone has his double somewhere in the world." Previously the Count had been discussing Planchette—he was a great authority on the supernatural, the sub-conscious, and the subliminal. He now deviated gracefully to the discussion of the theory of doubles.

"I suppose you aren't going out for a walk, dear, before dinner?" said Eve to Kitty.

"No, dear," said Kitty, positively.

"I think I shall," said Eve.

And her glance at Cecil Thorold intimated in the plainest possible manner that she wished not only to have a companion for a stroll, but to leave Kitty and the Count in dual solitude.

"I shouldn't, if I were you, Miss Fincastle," Cecil remarked, with calm and studied blindness. "It's risky here in the evenings—with these canals exhaling miasma and mosquitoes and bracelets and all sorts of things."

"I will take the risk, thank you," said Eve, in an icy tone, and she haughtily departed; she would not cower before Cecil's millions. As for Cecil, he joined in the discussion of the theory of doubles.

III

On the next afternoon but one, policemen were still fishing, without success, for the bracelet, and raising from the ancient duct long-buried odours which threatened to destroy the inhabitants of the quay. (When Kitty Sartorius had hinted that perhaps the authorities might see their way to drawing off the water from the canal, the authorities had intimated that the death-rate of Bruges was already as high as convenient.) Nevertheless, though nothing had happened, the situation had somehow developed, and in such a manner that the bracelet itself was in danger of being partially forgotten; and of all places in Bruges, the situation had developed on the top of the renowned Belfry which dominates the Grande Place in particular and the city in general.

The summit of the Belfry is three hundred and fifty feet high, and it is reached by four hundred and two winding stone steps, each a separate menace to life and limb. Eve Fincastle had climbed those steps alone, perhaps in quest of the view at the top, perhaps in quest of spiritual calm. She had not been leaning over the parapet more than a minute before Cecil Thorold had appeared, his field-glasses slung over his shoulder. They had begun to talk a little, but nervously and only in snatches. The wind blew free up there among the forty-eight bells, but the social atmosphere was oppressive.

"The Count is a most charming man," Eve was saying, as if in defence of the Count.

"He is," said Cecil; "I agree with you."

"Oh, no, you don't, Mr. Thorold! Oh, no, you don't!"

Then there was a pause, and the twain looked down upon Bruges, with its venerable streets, its grass-grown squares, its waterways, and its innumerable monuments, spread out maplike beneath them in the mellow October sunshine. Citizens passed along the thoroughfare in the semblance of tiny dwarfs.

"If you didn't hate him," said Eve, "you wouldn't behave as you do."

"How do I behave, then?"

Eve schooled her voice to an imitation of jocularity—

"All Tuesday evening, and all day yesterday, you couldn't leave them alone. You know you couldn't."

Five minutes later the conversation had shifted.

"You actually saw the bracelet fall into the canal?" said Cecil.

"I actually saw the bracelet fall into the canal. And no one could have got it out while Kitty and I were away, because we weren't away half a minute."

But they could not dismiss the subject of the Count, and presently he was again the topic.

"Naturally it would be a good match for the Count—for *any* man," said Eve; "but then it would also be a good match for Kitty. Of course, he is not so rich as some people, but he is rich."

Cecil examined the horizon with his glasses, and then the streets near the Grand Place.

"Rich, is he? I'm glad of it. By the by, he's gone to Ghent for the day, hasn't he?"

"Yes, he went by the 9.27, and returns by the 4.38."

Another pause.

"Well," said Cecil at length, handing the glasses to Eve Fincastle, "kindly glance down there. Follow the line of the Rue St. Nicolas. You see the cream-coloured house with the enclosed courtyard? Now, do you see two figures standing together near a door—a man and a woman, the woman on the steps? Who are they?"

"I can't see very well," said Eve.

"Oh, yes, my dear lady, you can," said Cecil. "These glasses are the very best. Try again."

"They look like the Comte d'Avrec and Madame Lawrence," Eve murmured.

"But the Count is on his way from Ghent! I see the steam of the 4.38 over there. The curious thing is that the Count entered the house of Madame Lawrence, to whom he was introduced for the first time the day before yesterday, at ten o'clock this morning. Yes, it would be a very good match for the Count. When one comes to think of it, it usually is that sort of man that contrives to marry a brilliant and successful actress. There! He's just leaving, isn't he? Now let us descend and listen to the recital of his day's doings in Ghent—shall we?"

"You mean to insinuate," Eve burst out in sudden wrath, "that the Count is an—an *adventurer*, and that Madame Lawrence—Oh! Mr. Thorold!" She laughed condescendingly. "This jealousy is too absurd. Do you suppose I haven't noticed how impressed you were with Kitty at the Devonshire Mansion that night, and again at Ostend, and again here? You're simply carried away by jealousy; and you think because you are a millionaire you must have all you want. I haven't the slightest doubt that the Count—"

"Anyhow," said Cecil, "let us go down and hear about Ghent."

His eyes made a number of remarks (indulgent, angry, amused, protective, admiring, perspicacious, puzzled), too subtle for the medium of words.

They groped their way down to earth in silence, and it was in silence that they crossed the Grande Place. The Count was seated on the *terrasse* in front of the hotel, with a liqueur glass before him, and he was making graceful and expressive signs to Kitty Sartorius, who leaned her marvellous beauty out of a first-storey window. He greeted Cecil Thorold and Eve with an equal grace.

"And how is Ghent?" Cecil inquired.

"Did you go to Ghent, after all, Count?" Eve put in. The Comte d'Avrec looked from one to another, and then, instead of replying, he sipped at his glass. "No," he said, "I didn't go. The rather curious fact is that I happened to meet Madame Lawrence, who offered to show me her collection of lace. I have been an amateur of lace for some years, and really Madame Lawrence's collection is amazing. You have seen it? No? You should do so. I'm afraid I have spent most of the day there."

When the Count had gone to join Kitty in the drawing-room, Eve Fincastle looked victoriously at Cecil, as if to demand of him: "Will you apologise?"

"My dear journalist," Cecil remarked simply, "you gave the show away."

That evening the continued obstinacy of the bracelet, which still refused to be caught, began at last to disturb the birdlike mind of Kitty Sartorius. Moreover, the secret was out, and the whole town of Bruges was discussing the episode and the chances of success.

"Let us consult Planchette," said the Count. The proposal was received with enthusiasm by Kitty. Eve had disappeared.

Planchette was produced; and when asked if the bracelet would be recovered, it wrote, under the hands of Kitty and the Count, a trembling "Yes." When asked: "By whom?" it wrote a word which faintly resembled "Avrec."

The Count stated that he should personally commence dragging operations at sunrise. "You will see," he said, "I shall succeed."

"Let me try this toy, may I?" Cecil asked blandly, and, upon Kitty agreeing, he addressed Planchette in a clear voice: "Now, Planchette, who will restore the bracelet to its owner?"

And Planchette wrote "Thorold," but in characters as firm and regular as those of a copy-book.

"Mr. Thorold is laughing at us," observed the Count, imperturbably bland.

"How horrid you are, Mr. Thorold!" Kitty exclaimed.

IV

Of the four persons more or less interested in the affair, three were secretly active that night, in and out of the hotel. Only Kitty Sartorius, chief mourner for the bracelet, slept placidly in her bed. It was towards three o'clock in the morning that a sort of preliminary crisis was reached.

From the multiplicity of doors which ventilate its rooms, one would imagine that the average foreign hotel must have been designed immediately after its architect had been to see a Palais Royal farce, in which every room opens into every other room in every act. The Hôtel de la Grande Place was not peculiar in this respect; it abounded in doors. All the chambers on the second storey, over the public rooms, fronting the Place, communicated one with the next, but naturally most of the communicating doors were locked. Cecil Thorold and the Comte d'Avrec had each a bedroom and a sitting-room on that floor. The Count's sitting-room adjoined Cecil's; and the door between was locked, and the key in the possession of the landlord.

Nevertheless, at three a.m. this particular door opened noiselessly from Cecil's side, and Cecil entered the domain of the Count. The moon shone, and Cecil could plainly see not only the silhouette of the Belfry across the Place, but also the principal objects within the room. He noticed the table in the middle, the large easy-chair turned towards the hearth, the old-fashioned sofa; but not a single article did he perceive which might have been the personal property of the Count. He cautiously passed across the room through the moonlight to the door of the Count's bedroom, which apparently, to his immense surprise, was not only shut, but locked, and the key in the lock on the sitting-room side. Silently unlocking it, he entered the bedroom and disappeared. . . .

In less than five minutes he crept back into the Count's sitting-room, closed the door and locked it.

"Odd!" he murmured reflectively; but he seemed quite happy.

There was a sudden movement in the region of the hearth, and a form rose from the armchair. Cecil rushed to the switch and turned on the electric light. Eve Fincastle stood before him. They faced each other.

"What are you doing here at this time, Miss Fincastle?" he asked, sternly. "You can talk freely; the Count will not waken."

"I may ask you the same question," Eve replied, with cold bitterness.

"Excuse me. You may not. You are a woman. This is the Count's room—"

"You are in error," she interrupted him. "It is not the Count's room. It is mine. Last night I told the Count I had some important writing to do, and I asked him as a favour to relinquish this room to me for twenty-four hours. He very kindly consented. He removed his belongings, handed me the key of that door, and the transfer was made in the hotel books. And now," she added, "may I inquire, Mr. Thorold, what you are doing in my room?"

"I—I thought it was the Count's," Cecil faltered decidedly at a loss for a moment. "In offering my humblest apologies, permit me to say that I admire you, Miss Fincastle."

"I wish I could return the compliment," Eve exclaimed, and she repeated with almost plaintive sincerity: "I do wish I could."

Cecil raised his arms and let them fall to his side.

"You meant to catch me," he said. "You suspected something, then? The 'important writing' was an invention." And he added, with a faint smile: "You really ought not to have fallen asleep. Suppose I had not wakened you?"

"Please don't laugh, Mr. Thorold. Yes, I did suspect. There was something in the demeanour of your servant Lecky that gave me the idea. . . . I did mean to catch you. Why you, a millionaire, should be a burglar, I cannot understand. I never understood that incident at the Devonshire Mansion; it was beyond me. I am by no means sure that you didn't have a great deal to do with the Rainshore affair at Ostend. But that you should have stooped to slander is the worst. I confess you are a mystery. I confess that I can make no guess at the nature of your present scheme. And what I shall do, now that I have caught you, I don't know. I can't decide; I must think. If, however, anything is missing to-morrow morning, I shall be bound in any case to denounce you. You grasp that?"

"I grasp it perfectly, my dear journalist," Cecil replied. "And something will not improbably be missing. But take the advice of a burglar and a mystery, and go to bed, it is half past three."

And Eve went. And Cecil bowed her out and then retired to his own rooms. And the Count's apartment was left to the moonlight.

V

"Planchette is a very safe prophet," said Cecil to Kitty Sartorius the next morning, "provided it has firm guidance."

They were at breakfast.

"What do you mean?"

"I mean that Planchette prophesied last night that I should restore to you your bracelet. I do."

He took the lovely gewgaw from his pocket and handed it to Kitty.

"Ho-ow did you find it, you dear thing?" Kitty stammered, trembling under the shock of joy.

"I fished it up out—out of the mire by a contrivance of my own."

"But when?"

"Oh! Very early. At three o'clock a.m. You see, I was determined to be first."

"In the dark, then?"

"I had a light. Don't you think I'm rather clever?"

Kitty's scene of ecstatic gratitude does not come into the story. Suffice it to say that not until the moment of its restoration did she realise how precious the bracelet was to her.

It was ten o'clock before Eve descended. She had breakfasted in her room, and Kitty had already exhibited to her the prodigal bracelet.

"I particularly want you to go up the Belfry with me, Miss Fincastle," Cecil greeted her; and his tone was so serious and so urgent that she consented. They left Kitty playing waltzes on the piano in the drawing-room.

"And now, O man of mystery?" Eve questioned, when they had toiled to the summit, and saw the city and its dwarfs beneath them.

"We are in no danger of being disturbed here," Cecil began; "but I will make my explanation—the explanation which I certainly owe you—as brief as possible. Your Comte d'Avrec is an adventurer (please don't be angry), and your Madame Lawrence is an adventuress. I knew that I had seen them together. They work in concert; and for the most part make a living on the gaming-tables of Europe. Madame Lawrence was expelled from Monte Carlo last year for being too intimate with a croupier. You may be aware that at a roulette-table one can do a great deal with the aid of the croupier. Madame Lawrence appropriated the bracelet 'on her own,' as it were. The Count (he may be a real Count, for anything I know) heard first of that enterprise from the lips of Miss Sartorius. He was annoyed, angry—because he was really a little in love with your friend, and he saw golden prospects. It is just this fact— the Count's genuine passion for Miss Sartorius—that renders the case psychologically interesting. To proceed, Madame Lawrence became jealous. The Count spent six hours yesterday in trying to get the bracelet from her, and failed. He tried again last night, and succeeded, but not too easily, for he did not re-enter the hotel till after one o'clock. At first I thought he had succeeded in the day-time, and I had arranged accordingly, for I did not see why he should have the honour and glory of restoring the bracelet to its owner. Lecky and I fixed up a sleeping-draught for him. The minor details were simple. When you caught me this morning, the bracelet was in my pocket, and in its stead I had left a brief note for the perusal of the Count, which has had the singular effect of inducing him to decamp; probably he has not gone alone. But isn't it amusing that, since you so elaborately took his sitting-room, he will be convinced that you are a party to his undoing—you, his staunchest defender?"

Eve's face gradually broke into an embarrassed smile.

"You haven't explained," she said, "how Madame Lawrence got the bracelet."

"Come over here," Cecil answered. "Take these glasses and look down at the Quai du Rosaire. You see everything plainly?" Eve could, in fact, see on the quay the little mounds of mud which had been extracted from the canal in the quest of the bracelet. Cecil continued: "On my arrival in Bruges on Monday, I had a fancy to climb the Belfry at once. I witnessed the whole scene between you and Miss Sartorius and Madame Lawrence, through my glasses. Immediately your backs were turned, Madame Lawrence, her hands behind her, and her back against the railing, began to make a sort of rapid, drawing up motion with her forearms. Then I saw a momentary glitter. . . . Considerably mystified, I visited the spot after you had left it, chatted with the gendarme on duty and got round him, and then it dawned on me that a robbery had been planned, prepared, and executed with extraordinary originality and ingenuity. A long, thin thread of black silk must have been ready tied to the railing, with perhaps a hook at the other end. As soon as Madame Lawrence held the bracelet, she attached the hook to it and dropped it. The silk, especially as it was the last thing in the world you would look for, would be as good as invisible. When you went for the police, Madame retrieved the bracelet, hid it in her muff, and broke off the silk. Only, in her haste, she left a bit of silk tied to the railing. That fragment I carried to the hotel. All along she must have been a little uneasy about me. . . . And that's all. Except that I wonder you thought I was jealous of the Count's attentions to your friend." He gazed at her admiringly.

"I'm glad you are not a thief, Mr. Thorold," said Eve.

"Well," Cecil smiled, "as for that, I left him a couple of louis for fares, and I shall pay his hotel bill."

"Why?"

"There were notes for nearly ten thousand francs with the bracelet. Ill-gotten gains, I am sure. A trifle, but the only reward I shall have for my trouble. I shall put them to good use." He laughed, serenely gay.

A Solution of the Algiers Mystery

I

"And the launch?"

"I am unaware of the precise technical term, sir, but the launch awaits you. Perhaps I should have said it is alongside."

The reliable Lecky hated the sea; and when his master's excursions became marine, he always squinted more formidably and suddenly than usual, and added to his reliability a certain quality of ironic bitterness.

"My overcoat, please," said Cecil Thorold, who was in evening dress.

The apartment, large and low, was panelled with bird's-eye maple; divans ran along the walls, and above the divans orange curtains were drawn; the floor was hidden by the skins of wild African animals; in one corner was a Steinway piano, with the score of "The Orchid" open on the music-stand; in another lay a large, flat bowl filled with blossoms that do not bloom in England; the illumination, soft and yellow, came from behind the cornice of the room, being reflected therefrom downwards by the cream-coloured ceiling. Only by a faintly-heard tremor of some gigantic but repressed force, and by a very slight unsteadiness on the part of the floor, could you have guessed that you were aboard a steam-yacht and not in a large, luxurious house.

Lecky, having arrayed the millionaire in overcoat, muffler, crush-hat, and white gloves, drew aside a *portière* and followed him up a flight of stairs. They stood on deck, surrounded by the

mild but treacherous Algerian night. From the white double fun-
nels a thin smoke oozed. On the white bridge, the second mate, a
spectral figure, was testing the engine-room signals, and the sharp
noise of the bell seemed to desecrate the mysterious silence of the
bay; but there was no other sign of life; the waiting launch was
completely hidden under the high bows of the *Claribel*. In distant
regions of the deck, glimmering beams came oddly up from below,
throwing into relief some part of a boat on its davits or a section of
a mast.

Cecil looked about him, at the serried lights of the Boulevard
Carnot, and the riding lanterns of the vessels in the harbour. Away
to the left on the hill, a few gleams showed Mustapha Supérieure,
where the great English hotels are; and ten miles further east, the
lighthouse on Cape Matifou flashed its eternal message to the Mediterranean. He was on the verge of feeling poetic.

"Suppose anything happens while you are at this dance, sir?"

Lecky jerked his thumb in the direction of a small steamer
which lay moored scarcely a cable's-length away, under the eastern jetty. "Suppose—?" He jerked his thumb again in exactly the
same direction. His tone was still pessimistic and cynical.

"You had better fire our beautiful brass cannon," Cecil replied.
"Have it fired three times. I shall hear it well enough up at Mustapha."

He descended carefully into the launch, and was whisked
puffingly over the dark surface of the bay to the landing-stage,
where he summoned a fiacre.

"Hotel St. James," he instructed the driver.

And the driver smiled joyously; everyone who went to the Hotel St. James was rich and lordly, and paid well, because the hill
was long and steep and so hard on the poor Algerian horses.

II

Every hotel up at Mustapha Supérieure has the finest view, the
finest hygienic installation, and the finest cooking in Algeria; in
other words, each is better than all the others. Hence the Hotel St.

James could not be called "first among equals," since there are no
equals, and one must be content to describe it as first among the
unequalled. First it undoubtedly was—and perhaps will be again.
Although it was new, it had what one visitor termed "that indefin-
able thing—*cachet*." It was frequented by the best people—namely,
the richest people, the idlest people, the most arrogant people, the
most bored people, the most titled people—that came to the southern shores of the Mediterranean in search of what they would never
find—an escape from themselves. It was a vast building, planned
on a scale of spaciousness only possible in a district where commercial crises have depressed the value of land, and it stood in the
midst of a vast garden of oranges, lemons, and medlars. Every
room—and there were three storeys and two hundred rooms—faced
south: this was charged for in the bill. The public rooms, Oriental
in character, were immense and complete. They included a dining-
room, a drawing-room, a reading-room, a smoking-room, a billiard-
room, a bridge-room, a ping-pong-room, a concert-room (with resi-
dent orchestra), and a room where Aissouias, negroes, and other
curiosities from the native town might perform before select par-
ties. Thus it was entirely self-sufficient, and lacked nothing which
is necessary to the proper existence of the best people. On Thursday nights, throughout the season, there was a five-franc dance in
the concert-hall. You paid five francs, and ate and drank as much
as you could while standing up at the supper-tables arrayed in the
dining-room.

On a certain Thursday night in early January, this Anglo-Saxon
microcosm, set so haughtily in a French colony between the Mediterranean and the Djujura Mountains (with the Sahara behind),
was at its most brilliant. The hotel was crammed, the prices were
high, and everybody was supremely conscious of doing the correct
thing. The dance had begun somewhat earlier than usual, because
the eagerness of the younger guests could not be restrained. And
the orchestra seemed gayer, and the electric lights brighter, and
the toilettes more resplendent that night. Of course, guests came
in from the other hotels. Indeed, they came in to such an extent
that to dance in the ballroom was an affair of compromise and

ingenuity. And the other rooms were occupied, too. The bridge players recked not of Terpsichore, the cheerful sound of ping-pong came regularly from the ping-pong-room; the retired Indian judge was giving points as usual in the billiard-room; and in the reading room the steadfast intellectuals were studying the *World* and the Paris *New York Herald*.

And all was English and American, pure Anglo-Saxon in thought and speech and gesture—save the manager of the hotel, who was Italian, the waiters, who were anything, and the wonderful concierge, who was everything.

As Cecil passed through the imposing suite of public rooms, he saw in the reading-room—posted so that no arrival could escape her eye—the elegant form of Mrs. Macalister, and, by way of a wild, impulsive freak, he stopped and talked to her, and ultimately sat down by her side.

Mrs. Macalister was one of those Englishwomen that are to be found only in large and fashionable hotels. Everything about her was mysterious, except the fact that she was in search of a second husband. She was tall, pretty, dashing, daring, well-dressed, well-informed, and, perhaps thirty-four. But no one had known her husband or her family, and no one knew her county, or the origin of her income, or how she got herself into the best cliques in the hotel. She had the air of being the merriest person in Algiers; really, she was one of the saddest, for the reason that every day left her older, and harder, and less likely to hook—well, to hook a millionaire. She had met Cecil Thorold at the dance of the previous week, and had clung to him so artfully that the coteries talked of it for three days, as Cecil well knew. And to-night he thought he might, as well as not, give Mrs. Macalister an hour's excitement of the chase, and the coteries another three days' employment.

So he sat down beside her, and they talked.

First she asked him whether he slept on his yacht or in the hotel; and he replied, sometimes in the hotel and sometimes on the yacht. Then she asked him where his bedroom was, and he said it was on the second floor, and she settled that it must be three doors from her own. Then they discussed bridge, the Fiscal Inquiry, the weather, dancing, food, the responsibilities of great wealth, Algerian railway-travelling, Cannes, gambling, Mr. Morley's "Life of Gladstone," and the extraordinary success of the hotel. Thus, quite inevitably, they reached the subject of the Algiers Mystery. During the season, at any rate, no two guests in the hotel ever talked small-talk for more than ten minutes without reaching the subject of the Algiers mystery.

For the hotel had itself been the scene of the Algiers Mystery, and the Algiers Mystery was at once the simplest, the most charming, and the most perplexing mystery in the world. One morning, the first of April in the previous year, an honest John Bull of a guest had come down to the hotel-office, and laying a five-pound note before the head clerk, had exclaimed: "I found that lying on my dressing-table. It isn't mine. It looks good enough, but I expect it's someone's joke." Seven other people that day confessed that they had found five-pound notes in their rooms, or pieces of paper that resembled five-pound notes. They compared these notes, and then the eight went off in a body down to an agency in the Boulevard de la République, and without the least demur the notes were changed for gold. On the second of April, twelve more people found five-pound notes in their rooms, now prominent on the bed, now secreted—as, for instance, under a candlestick. Cecil himself had been a recipient. Watches were set, but with no result whatever. In a week nearly seven hundred pounds had been distributed amongst the guests by the generous, invisible ghosts. It was magnificent, and it was very soon in every newspaper in England and America. Some of the guests did not "care" for it; thought it "queer," and "uncanny," and not "nice," and these left. But the majority cared for it very much indeed, and remained till the utmost limit of the Season.

The rainfall of notes had not recommenced so far, in the present Season. Nevertheless, the hotel had been thoroughly well patronised from November onwards, and there was scarcely a guest but who went to sleep at night hoping to descry a fiver in the morning.

"Advertisement!" said some perspicacious individuals. Of course, the explanation was an obvious one. But the manager had indignantly and honestly denied all knowledge of the business, and, moreover, not a single guest had caught a single note in the act of settling down. Further, the hotel changed hands and that manager left. The mystery, therefore, remained, a delightful topic always at hand for discussion.

After having chatted, Cecil Thorold and Mrs. Macalister danced—two dances. And the hotel began audibly to wonder that Cecil could be such a fool. When, at midnight, he retired to bed, many mothers of daughters and daughters of mothers were justifiably angry, and consoled themselves by saying that he had disappeared in order to hide the shame which must have suddenly overtaken him. As for Mrs. Macalister, she was radiant.

Safely in his room, Cecil locked and wedged the door, and opened the window and looked out from the balcony at the starry night. He could hear cats playing on the roof. He smiled when he thought of the things Mrs. Macalister had said, and of the ardour of her glances. Then he felt sorry for her. Perhaps it was the whisky-and-soda which he had just drunk that momentarily warmed his heart towards the lonely creature. Only one item of her artless gossip had interested him—a statement that the new Italian manager had been ill in bed all day.

He emptied his pockets, and, standing on a chair, he put his pocket-book on the top of the wardrobe, where no Algerian marauder would think of looking for it; his revolver he tucked under his pillow. In three minutes he was asleep.

III

He was awakened by a vigorous pulling and shaking of his arm; and he, who usually woke wide at the least noise, came to his senses with difficulty. He looked up. The electric light had been turned on.

"There's a ghost in my room, Mr. Thorold! You'll forgive me— but I'm so—"

It was Mrs. Macalister, dishevelled and in white, who stood over him.

"This is really a bit too thick," he thought vaguely and sleepily, regretting his impulsive flirtation of the previous evening. Then he collected himself and said sternly, severely, that if Mrs. Macalister would retire to the corridor, he would follow in a moment; he added that she might leave the door open if she felt afraid. Mrs. Macalister retired, sobbing, and Cecil arose. He went first to consult his watch; it was gone—a chronometer worth a couple of hundred pounds. He whistled, climbed on to a chair, and discovered that his pocket-book was no longer in a place of safety on the top of the wardrobe; it had contained something over five hundred pounds in a highly negotiable form. Picking up his overcoat, which lay on the floor, he found that the fur lining—a millionaire's fancy, which had cost him nearly a hundred and fifty pounds—had been cut away, and was no more to be seen. Even the revolver had departed from under his pillow!

"Well!" he murmured, "this is decidedly the grand manner."

Quite suddenly it occurred to him, as he noticed a peculiar taste in his mouth, that the whisky-and-soda had contained more than whisky-and-soda—he had been drugged! He tried to recall the face of the waiter who had served him. Eyeing the window and the door, he argued that the thief had entered by the former and departed by the latter. "But the pocket-book!" he mused. "I must have been watched!"

Mrs. Macalister, stripped now of all dash and all daring, could be heard in the corridor.

"Can she—?" He speculated for a moment, and then decided positively in the negative. Mrs. Macalister could have no design on anything but a bachelor's freedom.

He assumed his dressing-gown and slippers and went to her. The corridor was in darkness, but she stood in the light of his doorway.

"Now," he said, "this ghost of yours, dear lady!"

"You must go first," she whimpered. "I daren't. It was white. . . . but with a black face. It was at the window."

Cecil, getting a candle, obeyed. And having penetrated alone into the lady's chamber, he perceived, to begin with, that a pane had been pushed out of the window by the old, noiseless device of a sheet of treacled paper, and then, examining the window more closely, he saw that, outside, a silk ladder depended from the roof and trailed in the balcony.

"Come in without fear," he said to the trembling widow. "It must have been someone with more appetite than a ghost that you saw. Perhaps an Arab."

She came in, femininely trusting to him; and between them they ascertained that she had lost a watch, sixteen rings, an opal necklace, and some money. Mrs. Macalister would not say how much money. "My resources are slight," she remarked, "I was expecting remittances."

Cecil thought: "This is not merely in the grand manner. If it fulfils it promise, it will prove to be one of the greatest things of the age."

He asked her to keep cool, not to be afraid, and to dress herself. Then he returned to his room and dressed as quickly as he could. The hotel was absolutely quiet, but out of the depths below came the sound of a clock striking four. When, adequately but not æsthetically attired, he opened his door again, another door near by also opened, and Cecil saw a man's head.

"I say," drawled the man's head, "excuse me, but have *you* noticed anything?"

"Why? What?"

"Well, I've been robbed!"

The Englishman laughed awkwardly, apologetically, as though ashamed to have to confess that he had been victimised.

"Much?" Cecil inquired.

"Two hundred or so. No joke, you know."

"So have I been robbed," said Cecil. "Let us go downstairs. Got a candle? These corridors are usually lighted all night."

"Perhaps our thief has been at the switches," said the Englishman.

"Say our thieves," Cecil corrected.

"You think there was more than one?"

"I think there were more than half a dozen," Cecil replied.

The Englishman was dressed, and the two descended together, candles in hand, forgetting the lone lady. But the lone lady had no intention of being forgotten, and she came after them, almost screaming. They had not reached the ground floor before three other doors had opened and three other victims proclaimed themselves.

Cecil led the way through the splendid saloons, now so ghostly in their elegance, which only three hours before had been the illuminated scene of such polite revelry. Ere he reached the entrance-hall, where a solitary jet was burning, the assistant-concierge (one of those officials who seem never to sleep) advanced towards him, demanding in his broken English what was the matter.

"There have been thieves in the hotel," said Cecil. "Waken the concierge."

From that point, events succeeded each other in a sort of complex rapidity. Mrs. Macalister fainted at the door of the billiard-room and was laid out on a billiard-table, with a white ball between her shoulders. The head concierge was not in his narrow bed in the alcove by the main entrance, and he could not be found. Nor could the Italian manager be found (though he was supposed to be ill in bed), nor the Italian manager's wife. Two stablemen were searched out from somewhere; also a cook. And then the Englishman who had lost two hundred or so went forth into the Algerian night to bring a gendarme from the post in the Rue d'Isly.

Cecil Thorold contented himself with talking to people as, in ones and twos, and in various stages of incorrectness, they came into the public rooms, now brilliantly lighted. All who came had been robbed. What surprised him was the slowness of the hotel to wake up. There were two hundred and twenty guests in the place. Of these, in a quarter of an hour, perhaps fifteen had risen. The remainder were apparently oblivious of the fact that something very extraordinary, and something probably very interesting to them personally, had occurred and was occurring.

"Why! It's a conspiracy, sir. It's a conspiracy, that's what it is!" decided the Indian judge.

"Gang is a shorter word," Cecil observed, and a young girl in a macintosh giggled.

Sleepy *employés* now began to appear, and the rumour ran that six waiters and a chambermaid were missing. Mrs. Macalister rallied from the billiard table and came into the drawing-room, where most of the company had gathered. Cecil yawned (the influence of the drug was still upon him) as she approached him and weakly spoke. He answered absently; he was engaged in watching the demeanour of these idlers on the face of the earth—how incapable they seemed of any initiative, and yet with what magnificent Britannic phlegm they endured the strange situation! The talking was neither loud nor impassioned.

Then the low, distant sound of a cannon was heard. Once, twice, thrice.

Silence ensued.

"Heavens!" sighed Mrs. Macalister, swaying towards Cecil. "What can that be?"

He avoided her, hurried out of the room, and snatched somebody else's hat from the hat-racks in the hall. But just as he was turning the handle of the main door of the hotel, the Englishman who had lost two hundred or so returned out of the Algerian night with an inspector of police. The latter courteously requested Cecil not to leave the building, as he must open the inquiry (*ouvrir l'enquête*) at once. Cecil was obliged, regretfully, to comply.

The inspector of police then commenced his labours. He telephoned (no one had thought of the telephone) for assistance and asked the Central Bureau to watch the railway station, the port, and the stage coaches. He acquired the names and addresses of *tout le monde*. He made catalogues of articles. He locked all the servants in the ping-pong-room. He took down narratives, beginning with Cecil's. And while the functionary was engaged with Mrs. Macalister, Cecil quietly but firmly disappeared.

After his departure, the affair loomed larger and larger in mere magnitude, but nothing that came to light altered its leading characteristics. A wholesale robbery had been planned with the most minute care and knowledge, and executed with the most daring skill. Some ten persons—the manager and his wife, a chambermaid, six waiters, and the concierge—seemed to have been concerned in the enterprise, excluding Mrs. Macalister's Arab and no doubt other assistants. (The guests suddenly remembered how superior the concierge and the waiters had been to the ordinary concierge and waiter!) At a quarter past five o'clock the police had ascertained that a hundred rooms had been entered, and horrified guests were still descending! The occupants of many rooms, however, made no response to a summons to awake. These, it was discovered after- wards, had either, like Cecil, received a sedative unawares, or they had been neatly gagged and bound. In the result, the list of miss- ing valuables comprised nearly two hundred watches, eight hun- dred rings, a hundred and fifty other articles of jewellery, several thousand pounds' worth of furs, three thousand pounds in coin, and twenty-one thousand pounds in banknotes and other forms of currency. One lady, a doctor's wife, said she had been robbed of eight hundred pounds in Bank of England notes, but her story ob- tained little credit; other tales of enormous loss, chiefly by women, were also taken with salt. When the dawn began, at about six o'clock, an official examination of the facade of the hotel indicated that nearly every room had been invaded by the balconied win- dow, either from the roof or from the ground. But the stone flags of the terrace, and the beautifully asphalted pathways of the gar- den disclosed no trace of the plunderers.

"I guess your British habit of sleeping with the window open don't cut much ice to-day, anyhow!" said an American from In- dianapolis to the company.

That morning no omnibus from the hotel arrived at the station to catch the six-thirty train which takes two days to ramble to Tunis and to Biskra. And all the liveried porters talked together in ex- cited Swiss-German.

IV

"My compliments to Captain Black," said Cecil Thorold, "and repeat to him that all I want him to do is to keep her in sight. He needn't overhaul her too much."

"Precisely, sir." Lecky bowed; he was pale.

"And you had better lie down."

"I thank you, sir, but I find a recumbent position inconvenient. Perpetual motion seems more agreeable."

Cecil was back in the large, low room panelled with bird's-eye maple. Below him the power of two thousand horses drove through the nocturnal Mediterranean swell his *Claribel* of a thousand tons. Thirty men were awake and active on board her, and twenty slept in the vast, clean forecastle, with electric lights blazing six inches above their noses. He lit a cigarette, and going to the piano, struck a few chords from "The Orchid"; but since the music would not remain on the stand, he abandoned that attempt and lay down on a divan to think.

He had reached the harbour, from the hotel, in twenty minutes, partly on foot at racing speed, and partly in an Arab cart, also at racing speed. The *Claribel's* launch awaited him, and in another five minutes the launch was slung to her davits, and the *Claribel* under way. He learnt that the small and sinister vessel, the *Perroquet Vert* (of Oran), which he and his men had been watching for several days, had slipped unostentatiously between the southern and eastern jetties, had stopped for a few minutes to hold converse with a boat that had put off from the neighbourhood of Lower Mustapha, and had then pointed her head north-west, as though for some port in the province of Oran or in Morocco.

And in the rings of cigarette smoke which he made, Cecil seemed now to see clearly the whole business. He had never relaxed his interest in the affair of the five-pound notes. He had vaguely suspected it to be part of some large scheme; he had presumed, on slight grounds, a connection between the *Perroquet Vert* and the Italian manager of the hotel. Nay, more, he had felt sure that some great stroke was about to be accomplished. But of precise knowledge, of satisfactory theory, of definite expectation, he had had none—until Mrs. Macalister, that unconscious and man-hunting agent of Destiny, had fortunately wakened him in the nick of time. Had it not been for his flirtation of the previous evening, he might still be asleep in his bed at the hotel. . . . He perceived the entire plan. The five-pound notes had been mysteriously scattered, certainly to advertise the hotel, but only to advertise it for a particular and colossal end, to fill it full and overflowing with fat victims. The situation had been thoroughly studied in all its details, and the task had been divided and allotted to various brains. Every room must have been examined, watched, and separately plotted against; the habits and idiosyncracy of every victim must have been individually weighed and considered. Nothing, no trifle, could have been forgotten. And then some supreme intelligence had drawn the threads together and woven them swiftly into the pattern of a single night, almost a single hour! . . . And the loot (Cecil could estimate it pretty accurately) had been transported down the hill to Mustapha Inférieure, tossed into a boat, and so to the *Perroquet Vert*. And the *Perroquet Vert*, with loot and looters on board, was bound, probably, for one of those obscure and infamous ports of Oran or Morocco—Tenez, Mostaganem, Beni Sar, Melilla, or the city of Oran, or Tangier itself! He knew something of the Spanish and Maltese dens of Oran and Tangier, the clearing-houses for stolen goods of two continents, and the impregnable refuge of scores of ingenious villains.

And when he reflected upon the grandeur and immensity of the scheme, so simple in its essence, and so leisurely in its achievement, like most grand schemes; when he reflected upon the imagination which had been necessary even to conceive it, and the generalship which had been necessary to its successful conclusion, he murmured admiringly—

"The man who thought of that and did it may be a scoundrel; but he is also an artist, and a great one!"

And just because he, Cecil Thorold, was a millionaire, and possessed a hundred-thousand-pound toy, which could do nineteen knots an hour, and cost fifteen hundred pounds a month to run, he was about to defeat that great artist and nullify that great scheme, and incidentally to retrieve his watch, his revolver, his fur, and his five hundred pounds. He had only to follow, and to warn one of the French torpedo-boats which are always patrolling the coast between Algiers and Oran, and the bubble would burst!

He sighed for the doomed artist; and he wondered what that victimised crowd of European loungers, who lounged sadly round the Mediterranean in winter, and sadly round northern Europe in summer, had done in their languid and luxurious lives that they should be saved, after all, from the pillage to which the great artist in theft had subjected them!

Then Lecky re-entered the state room.

"We shall have a difficulty in keeping the *Perroquet Vert* in sight, sir."

"What!" exclaimed Cecil. "That tub! That coffin! You don't mean she can do twenty knots?"

"Exactly, sir. Coffin! It—I mean she—is sinking."

Cecil ran on deck. Dawn was breaking over Matifou, and a faint, cold, grey light touched here and there the heaving sea. His captain spoke and pointed. Ahead, right ahead, less than a mile away, the *Perroquet Vert* was sinking by the stern, and even as they gazed at her, a little boat detached itself from her side in the haze of the morning mist; and she sank, disappeared, vanished amid a cloud of escaping steam. They were four miles north-east of Cape Caxine. Two miles further westward, a big Dominion liner, bound direct for Algiers from the New World, was approaching and had observed the catastrophe—for she altered her course. In a few minutes, the *Claribel* picked up the boat of the *Perroquet Vert*. It contained three Arabs.

V

The tale told by the Arabs (two of them were brothers, and all three came from Oran) fully sustained Cecil Thorold's theory of the spoliation of the hotel. Naturally they pretended at first to an entire innocence concerning the schemes of those who had charge of the *Perroquet Vert*. The two brothers, who were black with coal-dust when rescued, swore that they had been physically forced to work in the stokehold; but ultimately all three had to admit a knowledge of things which was decidedly incriminating, and all three got three years' imprisonment. The only part of the Algiers mystery which remained a mystery was the cause of the sinking of the *Perroquet Vert*. Whether she was thoroughly unseaworthy (she had been picked up cheap at Melilla), or whether someone (not on board) had deliberately arranged her destruction, perhaps to satisfy a Moorish vengeance, was not ascertained. The three Arabs could only be persuaded to say that there had been eleven Europeans and seven natives on the ship, and that they alone, by the mercy of Allah, had escaped from the swift catastrophe.

The hotel underwent an acute crisis, from which, however, it is emerging. For over a week a number of the pillaged guests discussed a diving enterprise of salvage. But the estimates were too high, and it came to nothing. So they all, Cecil included, began to get used to the idea of possessing irrecoverable property to the value of forty thousand pounds in the Mediterranean. A superb business in telegraphed remittances was done for several days. The fifteen beings who had accompanied the *Perroquet Vert* to the bottom were scarcely thought of, for it was almost universally agreed that the way of transgressors is, and ought to be, hard.

As for Cecil Thorold, the adventure, at first so full of the promise of joy, left him melancholy, until an unexpected sequel diverted the channel of his thoughts.

In the Capital of the Sahara

I

Mrs. Macalister turned with sudden eagerness and alarm towards Cecil Thorold—the crowd on the lawn in front of the railings was so dense that only heads could be moved—and she said excitedly—

"I'm sure I can see my ghost across there!"

She indicated with her agreeable snub nose the opposite side of the course.

"Your ghost?" Cecil questioned, puzzled for a moment by this extraordinary remark.

Then the Arab horsemen swept by in a cloud of dust and of thunder, and monopolised the attention of the lawn and the grand stand, and the *élite* of Biskra crammed thereon and therein. They had one more lap to accomplish for the Prix de la Ville.

Biskra is an oasis in the desert, and the capital of the Algerian Sahara. Two days' journey by train from Algiers, over the Djujura Ranges, it is the last outpost of the Algerian State Railways. It has a hundred and sixty thousand palm trees; but the first symptom of Biskra to be observed from the approaching first-class carriage is the chimney of the electric light plant. Besides the hundred and sixty thousand palm trees, it possesses half a dozen large hotels, five native villages, a fort, a huge barracks, a very ornamental town hall, shops for photographic materials, a whole street of dancing-girls, the finest winter climate in all Africa, and a gambling Casino. It is a unique thing in oases. It completely upsets the conventional

71

idea of an oasis as a pool of water bordered with a few date-palms, and the limitless desert all round! Nevertheless, though Biskra as much resembles Paris as it resembles the conventional idea of an oasis, it is genuine enough, and the limitless desert is, in fact, all around. You may walk out into the desert—and meet a motor-car manœuvring in the sand; but the sand remains the sand, and the desert remains the desert, and the Sahara, more majestic than the sea itself, refuses to be cheapened by the pneumatic tyres of a Mercedes, or the blue rays of the electric light, or the feet of English, French, and Germans wandering in search of novelty—it persists in being august.

Once a year, in February, Biskra becomes really and excessively excited, and the occasion is its annual two-day race-meeting. Then the tribes and their chieftains and their horses and their camels arrive magically out of the four corners of the desert and fill the oasis. And the English, French, and Germans arrive from the Mediterranean coast, with their trunks and their civilisation, and crowd the hotels till beds in Biskra are precious beyond rubies. And under the tropical sun, East and West meet magnificently in the afternoon on the racecourse to the north of the European re-serve. And the tribesmen, their scraggy steeds trailing superb horsecloths, are arranged in hundreds behind the motor-cars and landaus, with the *parimutuel* in full swing twenty yards away. And the dancing-girls, the renowned Ouled-Naïls, covered with gold coins and with muslin in high, crude, violent purples, greens, ver-milions, shriek and whinny on their benches just opposite the grand stand, where the Western women, arrayed in the toilettes of Worth, Doucet, and Redfern, quiz them through their glasses. And, fring-ing all, is a crowd of the adventurers and rascals of two continents, the dark and the light. And in the background the palms wave eter-nally in the breeze. And to the east the Aurès mountains, snow-capped, rise in hues of saffron and pale rose, like stage mountains, against the sapphire sky. And to the south a line of telegraph poles lessens and disappears over the verge into the inmost heart of the mysterious and unchangeable Sahara.

It was amid this singular scene that Mrs. Macalister made to Cecil Thorold her bizarre remark about a ghost.

"What ghost?" the millionaire repeated, when the horsemen had passed.

Then he remembered that on the famous night, now nearly a month ago, when the Hotel St. James at Algiers was literally sacked by an organised band of depredators, and valuables to the tune of forty thousand pounds disappeared, Mrs. Macalister had given the first alarm by crying out that there was a ghost in her room.

"Ah!" He smiled easily, condescendingly, to this pertinacious widow, who had been pursuing him, so fruitlessly, for four mortal weeks, from Algiers to Tunis, from Tunis back to Constantine, and from Constantine here to Biskra. "All Arabs look more or less alike, you know."

"But—"

"Yes," he said again. "They all look alike, to us, like Chinamen."

Considering that he himself, from his own yacht, had witnessed the total loss in the Mediterranean of the vessel which contained the plunder and the fleeing band of thieves; considering that his own yacht had rescued the only three survivors of that shipwreck, and that these survivors had made a full confession, and had, only two days since, been duly sentenced by the criminal court at Algiers—he did not feel inclined to minister to Mrs. Macalister's feminine fancies.

"Did you ever see an Arab with a mole on his chin?" asked Mrs. Macalister.

"No, I never did."

"Well, my Arab had a mole on his chin, and that is why I am sure it was he that I saw a minute ago—over there. No, he's gone now!"

The competing horsemen appeared round the bend for the last time, the dancing-girls whinnied in their high treble, the crowd roared, and the Prix de la Ville was won and lost. It was the final race on the card, and in the *mêlée* which followed, Cecil became separated from his adorer. She was to depart on the morrow by the six a.m. train, "Urgent business," she said. She had given up the chase of the millionaire. "Perhaps she's out of funds, poor thing!" he reflected. "Anyhow, I hope I may never see her again." As a matter of fact he never did see her again. She passed out of his life as casually as she had come into it.

He strolled slowly towards the hotel through the perturbed crowd of Arabs, Europeans, carriages, camels, horses and motor-cars. The mounted tribesmen were in a state of intense excitement, and were continually burning powder in that mad fashion which seems to afford a peculiar joy to the Arab soul. From time to time a tribesman would break out of the ranks of his clan, and, spur-ring his horse and dropping the reins on the animal's neck, would fire revolvers from both hands as he flew over the rough ground. It was unrivalled horsemanship, and Cecil admired immensely the manner in which, at the end of the frenzied performance, these men, drunk with powder, would wheel their horses sharply while at full gallop, and stop dead.

And then, as one man, who had passed him like a hurricane, turned, paused, and jogged back to his tribe, Cecil saw that he had a mole on his chin. He stood still to watch the splendid fellow, and he noticed something far more important than the mole—he per-ceived that the revolver in the man's right hand had a chased butt.

"I can't swear to it," Cecil mused. "But if that isn't my revolver, stolen from under my pillow at the Hotel St. James, Algiers, on the tenth of January last, my name is Norval, and not Thorold."

And the whole edifice of his ideas concerning the robbery at the Hotel de Paris began to shake.

"That revolver ought to be at the bottom of the Mediterranean," he said to himself; "and so ought Mrs. Macalister's man with the mole, according to the accepted theory of the crime and the story of the survivors of the shipwreck of the *Perroquet Vert*."

He walked on, keeping the man in sight.

"Suppose," he murmured— "suppose all that stuff isn't at the bottom of the Mediterranean after all?"

A hundred yards further on, he happened to meet one of the white-clad native guides attached to the Royal Hotel, where he had lunched. The guide saluted and offered service, as all the Biskra guides do on all occasions. Cecil's reply was to point out the man with the mole.

"You see him, Mahomet," said Cecil. "Make no mistake. Find out what tribe he belongs to, where he comes from, and where he sleeps in Biskra, and I will give you a sovereign. Meet me at the Casino to-night at ten."

Mahomet grinned an honest grin and promised to earn the sovereign.

Cecil stopped an empty landau and drove hurriedly to the station to meet the afternoon train from civilisation. He had arrived in Biskra that morning by road from El Kantara, and Lecky was coming by the afternoon train with the luggage. On seeing him, he gave that invaluable factotum some surprising orders.

In addition to Lecky, the millionaire observed among the passengers descending from the train two other people who were known to him; but he carefully hid himself from these ladies. In three minutes he had disappeared into the nocturnal whirl and uproar of Biskra, solely bent on proving or disproving the truth of a brand-new theory concerning the historic sack of the Hotel St. James.

But that night he waited in vain for Mahomet at the packed Casino, where the Arab chieftains and the English gentlemen, alike in their tremendous calm, were losing money at *petits chevaux* with all the imperturbability of stone statues.

II

Nor did Cecil see anything of Mahomet during the next day, and he had reasons for not making inquiries about him at the Royal Hotel. But at night, as he was crossing the deserted market, Mahomet came up to him suddenly out of nowhere, and, grinning the eternal, honest, foolish grin, said in his odd English—

"I have found—him."

"Where?"

"Come," said Mahomet, mysteriously. The Eastern guide loves to be mysterious.

Cecil followed him far down the carnivalesque street of the Ouled-Nailg, where tom-toms and nameless instruments of music sounded from every other house, and the *premières danseuses* of the Sahara showed themselves gorgeously behind grilles, like beautiful animals in cages. Then Mahomet entered a crowded *café*, passed through it, and pushing aside a suspended mat at the other end, bade Cecil proceed further. Cecil touched his revolver (his new revolver), to make sure of its company, and proceeded further. He found himself in a low Oriental room, lighted by an odorous English lamp with a circular wick, and furnished with a fine carpet and two bedroom chairs certainly made in Curtain Road, Shoreditch—a room characteristic of Biskra. On one chair sat a man. But this person was not Mrs. Macalister's man with a mole. He was obviously a Frenchman, by his dress, gestures, and speech. He greeted the millionaire in French and then dropped into English—excellently grammatical and often idiomatic English, spoken with a strong French accent. He was rather a little man, thin, grey, and vivacious.

"Give yourself the pain of sitting down," said the Frenchman. "I am glad to see you. You may be able to help us."

"You have the advantage of me," Cecil replied, smiling.

"Perhaps," said the Frenchman. "You came to Biskra yesterday, Mr. Thorold, with the intention of staying at the Royal Hotel, where rooms were engaged for you. But yesterday afternoon you went to the station to meet your servant, and you ordered him to return to Constastine with your luggage and to await your instructions there. You then took a handbag and went to the Casino Hotel, and you managed, by means of diplomacy and of money, to get a bed in the *salle à manger*. It was all they could do for you. You gave the name of Collins. Biskra, therefore, is not officially aware of the presence of Mr. Cecil Thorold, the millionaire; while Mr. Collins is free to carry on his researches, to appear and to disappear as it pleases him."

"Yes," Cecil remarked. "You have got that fairly right. But may I ask—"

"Let us come to business at once," said the Frenchman, politely interrupting him. "Is this your watch?"

He dramatically pulled a watch and chain from his pocket.

"It is," said Cecil, quietly. He refrained from embroidering the affirmative with exclamations. "It was stolen from my bedroom at the Hotel St. James, with my revolver, some fur, and a quantity of money, on the tenth of January."

"You are surprised to find it is not sunk in the Mediterranean?"

"Thirty hours ago I should have been surprised," said Cecil. "Now I am not."

"And why not now?"

"Because I have formed a new theory. But have the goodness to give me the watch."

"I cannot," said the Frenchman, graciously. "Not at present."

There was a pause. The sound of music was heard from the *café*.

"But, my dear sir, I insist." Cecil spoke positively.

The Frenchman laughed. "I will be perfectly frank with you, Mr. Thorold. Your cleverness in forming a new theory of the great robbery merits all my candour. My name is Sylvain, and I am head of the detective force of Algiers, *Chef de la Sureté*. You will perceive that I cannot part with the watch without proper formalities. Mr. Thorold, the robbery at the Hotel St. James was a work of the highest criminal art. Possibly I had better tell you the nature of our recent discoveries."

"I always thought well of the robbery," Cecil observed, "and my opinion of it is rising. Pray continue."

"According to your new theory, Mr. Thorold, how many persons were on board the *Perroquet Vert* when she began to sink?"

"Three," said Cecil promptly, as though answering a conundrum.

The Frenchman beamed. "You are admirable," he exclaimed. "Yes, instead of eighteen, there were three. The wreck of the *Perroquet Vert* was carefully pre-arranged; the visit of the boat to the *Perroquet Vert* off Mustapha Inférieure was what you call, I believe, a 'plant.' The stolen goods never left dry land. There were three Arabs only on the *Perroquet Vert*—one to steer her, and the other two in the engine-room. And these three were very careful to get themselves saved. They scuttled their ship in sight of your yacht and of another vessel. There is no doubt, Mr. Thorold," the Frenchman smiled with a hint of irony, "that the thieves were fully *au courant* of your doings on the *Claribel*. The shipwreck was done deliberately, with you and your yacht for an audience. It was a masterly stroke," he proceeded, almost enthusiastically, "for it had the effect, not merely of drawing away suspicion from the true direction, but of putting an end to all further inquiries. Were not the goods at the bottom of the sea, and the thieves drowned? What motive could the police have for further activity? In six months— nay, three months—all the notes and securities could be safely negotiated, because no measures would have to be taken to stop them. Why take measures to stop notes that are at the bottom of the sea?"

"But the three survivors who are now in prison," Cecil said. "Their behaviour, their lying, needs some accounting for."

"Quite simple," the Frenchman went on. "They are in prison for three years. What is that to an Arab? He will suffer it with stoicism. Say that ten thousand francs are deposited with each of their families. When they come out, they are rich for life. At a cost of thirty thousand francs and the price of the ship—say another thirty thousand—the thieves reasonably expected to obtain absolute security."

"It was a heroic idea!" said Cecil.

"It was," said the Frenchman. "But it has failed."

"Evidently. But why?"

"Can you ask? You know as well as I do! It has failed, partly because there were too many persons in the secret, partly because of the Arab love of display on great occasions, and partly because of a mole on a man's chin."

"By the way, that was the man I came here to see," Cecil remarked.

"He is arrested," said the Frenchman curtly, and then he sighed. "The booty was not guarded with sufficient restrictions. It was not kept in bulk. One thief probably said: 'I cannot do without this lovely watch.' And another said: 'What a revolver! I must have it.' Ah! The Arab, the Arab! The Europeans ought to have provided for that. That is where they were foolish—the idiots! The idiots!" he repeated angrily.

"You seem annoyed."

"Mr. Thorold, I am a poet in these things. It annoys me to see a fine composition ruined by bad construction in the fifth act. . . . However, as chief of the surety, I rejoice."

"You have located the thieves and the plunder?"

"I think I have. Certainly I have captured two of the thieves and several articles. The bulk lies at—" He stopped and looked round. "Mr. Thorold, may I rely on you? I know, perhaps more than you think of your powers. May I rely on you?"

"You may," said Cecil.

"You will hold yourself at my disposition during to-morrow, to assist me?"

"With pleasure."

"Then let us take coffee. In the morning, I shall have acquired certain precise information which at the moment I lack. Let us take coffee."

III

On the following morning, somewhat early, while walking near Mecid, one of the tiny outlying villages of the oasis, Cecil met Eve Fincastle and Kitty Sartorius, whom he had not spoken with since the affair of the bracelet at Bruges, though he had heard from them and had, indeed, seen them at the station two days before. Eve Fincastle had fallen rather seriously ill at Mentone, and the holiday of the two girls, which should have finished before the end of the year, was prolonged. Financially, the enforced leisure was a matter of trifling importance to Kitty Sartorius, who had insisted on remaining with her friend, much to the disgust of her London manager. But the journalist's resources were less royal, and Eve considered herself fortunate that she had obtained from her newspaper some special descriptive correspondence in Algeria. It was this commission which had brought her, and Kitty with her, in the natural course of an Algerian tour, to Biskra.

Cecil was charmed to see his acquaintances; for Eve interested him, and Kitty's beauty (it goes without saying) dazzled him. Nevertheless, he had been, as it were, hiding himself, and, in his character as an amateur of the loot of cities, he would have preferred to have met them on some morning other than that particular morning.

"You will go with us to Sidi Okba, won't you, to-day?" said Kitty, after they had talked a while. "We've secured a carriage, and I'm dying for a drive in the real, true desert."

"Sorry I can't," said Cecil.

"Oh, but—" Eve Fincastle began, and stopped.

"Of course you can," said Kitty imperiously. "You must. We leave to-morrow—we're only here for two days—for Algiers and France. Another two days in Paris, and then London, my darling London, and work! So it's understood?"

"It desolates me," said Cecil. "But I can't go with you to Sidi Okba to-day."

They both saw that he meant to refuse them.

"That settles it, then," Eve agreed quietly.

"You're horrid, Mr. Thorold," said the bewitching actress. "And if you imagine for a single moment we haven't seen that you've been keeping out of our way, you're mistaken. You must have noticed us at the station. Eve thinks you've got another of your—"

"No, I don't, Kitty," said Eve quickly.

"If Miss Fincastle suspects that I've got another of my—" he paused humorously, "Miss Fincastle is right. I *have* got another of my— I throw myself on your magnanimity. I am staying in Biskra under the name of Collins, and my time, like my name, is not my own."

"In that case," Eve remarked, "we will pass on."

And they shook hands, with a certain frigidity on the part of the two girls.

During the morning, M. Sylvain made no sign, and Cecil lunched in solitude at the Dar Eef, adjoining the Casino. The races being over, streams of natives, with their tents and their quadrupeds, were leaving Biskra for the desert; they made an interminable procession which could be seen from the window of the Dar Eef coffee room. Cecil was idly watching this procession, when a hand touched his shoulder. He turned and saw a gendarme.

"Monsieur Collang?" questioned the gendarme.

Cecil assented.

"*Voulez-vous avoir l'obligeance de me suivre, monsieur?*"

Cecil obediently followed, and found in the street M. Sylvain, well wrapped up, and seated in an open carriage.

"I have need of you," said M. Sylvain. "Can you come at once?"

"Certainly."

In two minutes they were driving away together into the desert.

"Our destination is Sidi Okba," said M. Sylvain. "A curious place."

The road (so called) led across the Biskra River (so called), and then in a straight line eastwards. The river had about the depth of a dinner plate. As for the road, in some parts it not only merely failed to be a road—it was nothing but virgin desert, intact: at its best it was a heaving and treacherous mixture of sand and pebbles, through which, and not over which, the two unhappy horses had to drag Sylvain's unfortunate open carriage.

M. Sylvain himself drove.

"I am well acquainted with this part of the desert," he said. "We have strange cases sometimes. And when I am on important business, I never trust an Arab. By the way, you have a revolver? I do not anticipate danger, but—"

"I have one," said Cecil.

"And it is loaded?"

Cecil took the weapon from his hip pocket and examined it.

"It is loaded," he said.

"Good!" exclaimed the Frenchman, and then he turned to the gendarme, who was sitting as impassively as the leaps and bounds of the carriage would allow, on a small seat immediately behind the other two, and demanded of him in French whether his revolver also was loaded. The man gave a respectful affirmative. "Good!"

exclaimed M. Sylvain again, and launched into a description of the wondrous gardens of the Comte Landon, whose walls, on the confines of the oasis, they were just passing.

Straight in front could be seen a short line of palm trees, waving in the desert breeze under the desert sun, and Cecil asked what they were.

"Sidi Okba," replied M. Sylvain. "The hundred and eighty thousand palms of the desert city of Sidi Okba. They seem near to you, no doubt, but we shall travel twenty kilometers before we reach them. The effect of nearness is due to the singular quality of the atmosphere. It is a two hours' journey."

"Then do we return in the dark?" Cecil inquired.

"If we are lucky, we may return at once, and arrive in Biskra at dusk. If not—well, we shall spend the night in Sidi Okba. You object?"

"Not at all."

"A curious place," observed M. Sylvain.

Soon they had left behind all trace of the oasis, and were in the "real, true desert." They met and passed native equipages and strings of camels, and from time to time on either hand at short distances from the road could be seen the encampments of wandering tribes. And after interminable joltings, in which M. Sylvain, his guest, and his gendarme were frequently hurled at each other's heads with excessive violence, the short line of palm trees began to seem a little nearer and to occupy a little more of the horizon. And then they could descry the wall of the city. And at last they reached its gate and the beggars squatting within its gate.

"Descend!" M. Sylvain ordered his subordinate.

The man disappeared, and M. Sylvain and Cecil drove into the city; they met several carriages of Biskra visitors just setting forth on the return journey.

In insisting that Sidi Okba was a curious place, M. Sylvain did not exaggerate. It is an Eastern town of the most antique sort, built solely of mud, with the simplicity, the foulness, the smells, and the avowed and the secret horrors which might be expected in a community which has not altered its habits in any particular for a thousand years. During several months of each year it is visited daily by Europeans (its mosque is the oldest Mohammedan building in Africa, therefore no respectable tourist dares to miss it), and yet it remains absolutely uninfluenced by European notions. The European person must take his food with him; he is allowed to eat it in the garden of a *café* which is European as far as its sign and its counter, but no further; he could not eat it in the *café* itself. This *café* is the mark which civilisation has succeeded in making on Sidi Okba in ten centuries.

As Cecil drove with M. Sylvain through the narrow, winding street, he acutely felt the East closing in upon him; and, since the sun was getting low over the palm trees, he was glad to have the detective by his side.

They arrived at the wretched *café*. A pair-horse vehicle, with the horses' heads towards Biskra, was waiting at the door. Unspeakable lanes, fetid, winding, sinister, and strangely peopled, led away in several directions.

M. Sylvain glanced about him.

"We shall succeed," he murmured cheerfully. "Follow me."

And they went into the mark of civilisation, and saw the counter, and a female creature behind the bar, and, through another door, a glimpse of the garden beyond.

"Follow me," murmured M. Sylvain again, opening another door to the left into a dark passage. "Straight on. There is a room at the other end."

They vanished.

In a few seconds M. Sylvain returned into the *café*.

IV

Now, in the garden were Eve Fincastle and Kitty Sartorius, tying up some wraps preparatory to their departure for Biskra. They caught sight of Cecil Thorold and his companion entering the *café*, and they were surprised to find the millionaire in Sidi Okba after his refusal to accompany them.

Through the back door of the *café* they saw Cecil's companion reappear out of the passage. They saw the creature behind the counter stoop and produce a revolver and then offer it to the Frenchman with a furtive movement. They saw that the Frenchman declined it, and drew another revolver from his own pocket and winked. And the character of the wink given by the Frenchman to the woman made them turn pale under the sudden, knife-like thrust of an awful suspicion.

The Frenchman looked up and perceived the girls in the garden, and one glance at Kitty's beauty was not enough for him.

"Can you keep him here a minute while I warn Mr. Thorold?" said Eve quickly.

Kitty Sartorius nodded and began to smile on the Frenchman; she then lifted her finger beckoningly. If millions had depended on his refusal, it is doubtful whether he would have resisted that charming gesture. (Not for nothing did Kitty Sartorius receive a hundred a week at the Regency Theatre.) In a moment the Frenchman was talking to her, and she had enveloped him in a golden mist of enchantment.

Guided by a profound instinct, Eve ran up the passage and into the room where Cecil was awaiting the return of his M. Sylvain.

"Come out," she whispered passionately, as if between violent anger and dreadful alarm. "You are trapped—you, with your schemes!"

"Trapped!" he exclaimed, smiling. "Not at all. I have my revolver!" His hand touched his pocket. "By Jove! I haven't! It's gone!"

The miraculous change in his face was of the highest interest.

"Come out!" she cried. "Our carriage is waiting!"

In the *café*, Kitty Sartorius was talking to the Frenchman. She stroked his sleeve with her gloved hand, and he, the Frenchman, still held the revolver which he had displayed to the woman of the counter.

Inspired by the consummate and swiftly aroused emotion of that moment, Cecil snatched at the revolver. The three friends walked hastily to the street, jumped into the carriage, and drove away. Already as they approached the city gate, they could see the white tower of the Royal Hotel at Biskra shining across the desert like a promise of security. . . .

The whole episode had lasted perhaps two minutes, but they were minutes of such intense and blinding revelation as Cecil had never before experienced. He sighed with relief as he lay back in the carriage.

"And that's the man," he meditated, astounded, "who must have planned the robbery of the Hotel St. James! And I never suspected it! I never suspected that his gendarme was a sham! I wonder whether his murder of me would have been as leisurely and artistic as his method of trapping me! I wonder! . . . Well, this time I have certainly enjoyed myself."

Then he gazed at Eve Fincastle.

The women said nothing for a long time, and even then the talk was of trifles.

V

Eve Fincastle had gone up on to the vast, flat roof of the Royal Hotel, and Cecil, knowing that she was there, followed. The sun had just set, and Biskra lay spread out below them in the rich evening light which already, eastwards, had turned to sapphire. They could still see the line of the palm trees of Sidi Okba, and in another direction, the long, lonely road to Figuig, stretching across the desert like a rope which had been flung from heaven on the waste of sand. The Aurès mountains were black and jagged. Nearer, immediately under them, was the various life of the great oasis, and the sounds of that life—human speech, the rattle of carriages, the grunts of camels in the camel enclosure, the whistling of an engine at the station, the melancholy wails of hawkers—ascended softly in the twilight of the Sahara.

Cecil approached her, but she did not turn towards him.

"I want to thank you," he started.

She made no movement, and then suddenly she burst out. "Why do you continue with these shameful plots and schemes?" she demanded, looking always steadily away from him. "Why do you disgrace yourself? Was this another theft, another blackmailing, another affair like that at Ostend? Why—" She stopped, deeply disturbed, unable to control herself.

"My dear journalist," he said quietly, "you don't understand. Let me tell you."

He gave her his history from the night summons by Mrs. Macalister to that same afternoon.

She faced him.

"I'm so glad," she murmured. "You can't imagine—"

"I want to thank you for saving my life," he said again.

She began to cry; her body shook; she hid her face.

"But—" he stammered awkwardly.

"It wasn't I who saved your life," she said, sobbing passionately. "I wasn't beautiful enough. Only Kitty could have done it. Only a beautiful woman could have kept that man—"

"I know all about it, my dear girl," Cecil silenced her disavowal. Something moved him to take her hand. She smiled sadly, not resisting. "You must excuse me," she murmured. "I'm not myself to-night. . . . It's because of the excitement. . . . Anyhow, I'm glad you haven't taken any 'loot' this time."

"But I have," he protested. (He was surprised to find his voice trembling.)

"What?"

"This." He pressed her hand tenderly.

"That?" She looked at her hand, lying in his, as though she had never seen it before.

"Eve," he whispered.

About two-thirds of the loot of the Hotel St. James was ultimately recovered; not at Sidi Okba, but in the cellars of the Hotel St. James itself. From first to last that robbery was a masterpiece of audacity. Its originator, the *soi-disant* M. Sylvain, head of the Algiers detective force, is still at large.

Lo! 'Twas a Gala Night!

I

Paris. And not merely Paris, but Paris *en fête*, Paris decorated, Paris idle, Paris determined to enjoy itself, and succeeding brilliantly. Venetian masts of red and gold lined the gay pavements of the *grands boulevarde* and the Avenue de l'Opéra; and suspended from these in every direction, transverse and lateral, hung garlands of flowers whose petals were of coloured paper, and whose hearts were electric globes that in the evening would burst into flame. The effect of the city's toilette reached the extreme of opulence, for no expense had been spared. Paris was welcoming monarchs, and had spent two million francs in obedience to the maxim that what is worth doing at all is worth doing well.

The Grand Hotel, with its eight hundred rooms full of English and Americans, at the upper end of the Avenue de l'Opéra, looked down at the Grand Hotel du Louvre, with its four hundred rooms full of English and Americans, at the lower end of the Avenue de l'Opéra. These two establishments had the best views in the whole city; and perhaps the finest view of all was that obtainable from a certain second floor window of the Grand Hotel, precisely at the corner of the Boulevard des Capucines and the Rue Auber. From this window one could see the boulevards in both directions, the Opéra, the Place de l'Opéra, the Avenue de l'Opéra, the Rue du Quatre Septembre, and the multitudinous life of the vivid thoroughfares—the glittering *cafés*, the dazzling shops, the painted *kiosks*, the lumbering omnibuses, the gliding trams, the hooting

87

automobiles, the swift and careless cabs, the private carriages, the suicidal bicycles, the newsmen, the toysellers, the touts, the beggars, and all the holiday crowd, sombre men and radiant women, chattering, laughing, bustling, staring, drinking, under the innumerable tricolours and garlands of paper flowers.

That particular view was a millionaire's view, and it happened to be the temporary property of Cecil Thorold, who was enjoying it and the afternoon sun at the open window, with three companions. Eve Fincastle looked at it with the analytic eye of the journalist, while Kitty Sartorius, as was quite proper for an actress, deemed it a sort of frame for herself, as she leaned over the balcony like a *Juliet* on the stage. The third guest in Cecil's sittingroom was Lionel Belmont, the Napoleonic Anglo-American theatrical manager, in whose crown Kitty herself was the chief star. Mr. Belmont, a big, burly, good-humoured, shrewd man of something over forty, said he had come to Paris on business. But for two days the business had been solely to look after Kitty Sartorius and minister to her caprices. At the present moment his share of the view consisted mainly of Kitty; in the same way Cecil's share of the view consisted mainly of Eve Fincastle; but this at least was right and decorous, for the betrothal of the millionaire and the journalist had been definitely announced. Otherwise Eve would have been back at work in Fleet Street a week ago.

"The gala performance is to-night, isn't it?" said Eve, gazing at the vast and superbly ornamented Opera House.

"Yes," said Cecil.

"What a pity we can't be there! I should so have liked to see the young Queen in evening dress. And they say the interior decorations—"

"Nothing simpler," said Cecil. "If you want to go, dear, let us go."

Kitty Sartorius looked round quickly. "Mr. Belmont has tried to get seats, and can't. Haven't you, Bel? You know the whole audience is invited. The invitations are issued by the Minister of Fine Arts."

"Still, in Paris, anything can be got by paying for it," Cecil insisted.

"My dear young friend," said Lionel Belmont, "I guess if seats were to be had, I should have struck one or two yesterday. I put no limit on the price, and I reckon I ought to know what theatre prices run to. Over at the Metropolitan in New York I've seen a box change hands at two thousand dollars, for one night."

"Nevertheless—" Cecil began again.

"And the performance starting in six hours from now!" Lionel Belmont exclaimed. "Not much!"

But Cecil persisted.

"Seen the *Herald* to-day?" Belmont questioned. "No? Well, listen. This will interest you." He drew a paper from his pocket and read: "Seats for the Opéra Gala. The traffic in seats for the gala performance at the Opéra during the last Royal Visit to Paris aroused considerable comment and not a little dissatisfaction. Nothing, however, was done, and the traffic in seats for to-night's spectacle, at which the President and their Imperial Majesties will be present, has, it is said, amounted to a scandal. Of course, the offer so suddenly made, five days ago, by Madame Félise and Mademoiselle Malva, the two greatest living dramatic sopranos, to take part in the performance, immediately and enormously intensified interest in the affair, for never yet have these two supreme artists appeared in the same theatre on the same night. No theatre could afford the luxury. Our readers may remember that in our columns and in the columns of the *Figaro* there appeared four days ago an advertisement to the following effect: '*A box, also two orchestra stalls, for the Opéra Gala, to be disposed of, owing to illness. Apply, 155, Rue de la Paix.*' We sent four several reporters to answer that advertisement. The first was offered a stage-box for seven thousand five hundred francs, and two orchestra stalls in the second row for twelve hundred and fifty francs. The second was offered a box opposite the stage on the second tier, and two stalls in the seventh row. The third had the chance of four stalls in the back row and a small box just behind them; the fourth was offered something else. The thing was obviously, therefore, a regular agency. Everybody is asking: 'How were these seats obtained? From the Ministry of Fine Arts, or from the *invités?*' *Echo* answers

'How?' The authorities, however, are stated to have interfered at last, and to have put an end to this buying and selling of what should be an honourable distinction."

"Bravo!" said Cecil.

"And that's so!" Belmont remarked, dropping the paper. "I went to 155, Rue de la Paix myself yesterday, and was told that nothing whatever was to be had, not at any price."

"Perhaps you didn't offer enough," said Cecil.

"Moreover, I notice the advertisement does not appear to-day. I guess the authorities have crumpled it up."

"Still—" Cecil went on monotonously.

"Look here," said Belmont, grim and a little nettled. "Just to cut it short, I'll bet you a two-hundred-dollar dinner at Paillard's that you can't get seats for to-night—not even two, let alone four."

"You really want to bet?"

"Well," drawled Belmont, with a certain irony, slightly imitating Cecil's manner, "it means something to eat for these ladies."

"I accept," said Cecil. And he rang the bell.

II

"Lecky," Cecil said to his valet, who had entered the room, "I want you to go to No. 155, Rue de la Paix, and find out on which floor they are disposing of seats for the Opéra to-night. When you have found out, I want you to get me four seats—preferably a box. Understand?"

The servant stared at his master, squinting violently for a few seconds. Then he replied suddenly, as though light had just dawned on him. "Exactly, sir. You intend to be present at the gala performance?"

"You have successfully grasped my intention," said Cecil. "Present my card." He scribbled a word or two on a card and gave it to the man.

"And the price, sir?"

"You still have that blank cheque on the Crédit Lyonnais that I gave you yesterday morning. Use that."

"Yes, sir. Then there is the question of my French, sir, my feeble French—a delicate plant."

"My friend," Belmont put in. "I will accompany you as interpreter. I should like to see this thing through."

Lecky bowed and gave up squinting.

In three minutes (for they had only to go round the corner), Lionel Belmont and Lecky were in a room on the fourth floor of 155, Rue de la Paix. It had the appearance of an ordinary drawing-room, save that it contained an office table; at this table sat a young man, French.

"You wish, messieurs?" said the young man.

"Have the goodness to interpret for me," said Lecky to the Napoleon of Anglo-Saxon theatres. "Mr. Cecil Thorold, of the Devonshire Mansion, London, the Grand Hotel, Paris; the Hôtel Continental, Rome, and the Ghezireh Palace Hotel, Cairo, presents his compliments, and wishes a box for the gala performance at the Opéra to-night."

Belmont translated, while Lecky handed the card.

"Owing to the unfortunate indisposition of a Minister and his wife," replied the young man gravely, having perused the card, "it happens that I have a stage-box on the second tier."

"You told me yesterday—" Belmont began.

"I will take it," said Lecky in a sort of French, interrupting his interpreter. "The price? And a pen."

"The price is twenty-five thousand francs."

"Gemini!" Belmont exclaimed in American. "This is Paris, and no mistake!"

"Yes," said Lecky, as he filled up the blank cheque, "Paris still succeeds in being Paris. I have noticed it before, Mr. Belmont, if you will pardon the liberty."

The young man opened a drawer and handed to Lecky a magnificent gilt card, signed by the Minister of Fine Arts, which Lecky hid within his breast.

"That signature of the Minister is genuine, eh?" Belmont asked the young man.

"I answer for it," said the young man, smiling imperturbably.

"The deuce you do!" Belmont murmured.

So the four friends dined at Paillard's at the rate of about a dollar and a-half a mouthful, and the mystified Belmont, who was not in the habit of being mystified, and so felt it, had the ecstasy of paying the bill.

III

It was nine o'clock when they entered the magnificent precincts of the Opera House. Like everybody else, they went very early—the performance was not to commence until nine-thirty—in order to see and be seen to the fullest possible extent. A week had elapsed since the two girls had arrived from Algiers in Paris, under the escort of Cecil Thorold, and in that time they had not been idle. Kitty Sartorius had spent tolerable sums at the best *modistes*, in the Rue de la Paix and the establishments in the Rue de la Chausée d'Antin, while Eve had bought one frock (a dream, needless to say), and had also been nearly covered with jewellery by her betrothed. That afternoon, between the bet and the dinner, Cecil had made more than one mysterious disappearance. He finally came back with a diamond tiara for his dear journalist. "You ridiculous thing!" exclaimed the dear journalist, kissing him. It thus occurred that Eve, usually so severe of aspect, had more jewels than she could wear, while Kitty, accustomed to display, had practically nothing but her famous bracelet. Eve insisted on pooling the lot, and dividing equally, for the gala.

Consequently, the party presented a very pretty appearance as it ascended the celebrated grand staircase of the Opéra, wreathed to-night in flowers. Lionel Belmont, with Kitty on his arm, was in high spirits, uplifted, joyous; but Cecil himself seemed to be a little nervous, and this nervousness communicated itself to Eve Fincastle—or perhaps Eve was rather overpowered by her tiara. At the head of the staircase was a notice requesting everyone to be seated at nine-twenty-five, previous to the arrival of the President and the Imperial guests of the Republic.

The row of officials at the *controle* took the expensive gilt card from Cecil, examined it, returned it, and bowed low with an intimation that he should turn to the right and climb two floors; and the party proceeded further into the interior of the great building. The immense corridors and *foyers* and stairs were crowded with a collection of the best-known people and the best-dressed people and the most wealthy people in Paris. It was a gathering of all the renowns. The garish, gorgeous Opéra seemed to be changed that night into something new and strange. Even those shabby old harridans, the box-openers, the *ouvreuses*, wore bows of red, white and blue, and smiled effusively in expectation of tips inconceivably large.

"*Tiens!*" exclaimed the box-opener who had taken charge of Cecil's party, as she unlocked the door of the box.

And well might she exclaim, for the box (No. 74—no possible error) was already occupied by a lady and two gentlemen, who were talking rather loudly in French! Cecil undoubtedly turned pale, while Lionel Belmont laughed within his moustache.

"These people have made a mistake," Cecil was saying to the *ouvreuse*, when a male official in evening dress approached him with an air of importance.

"Pardon, monsieur. You are Monsieur Cecil Thorold?"

"I am," said Cecil.

"Will you kindly follow me? Monsieur the Directeur wishes to see you."

"You are expected, evidently," said Lionel Belmont. The girls kept apart, as girls should in these crises between men.

"I have a ticket for this box," Cecil remarked to the official. "And I wish first to take possession of it."

"It is precisely that point which Monsieur the Directeur wishes to discuss with Monsieur," rejoined the official, ineffably suave. He turned with a wonderful bow to the girls, and added with that politeness of which the French alone have the secret: "Perhaps, in the meantime, these ladies would like to see the view of the Avenue de l'Opéra from the balcony? The illuminations have begun, and the effect is certainly charming."

Cecil bit his lip.

"Yes," he said. "Belmont, take them."

So, while Lionel Belmont escorted the girls to the balcony, there to discuss the startling situation and to watch the Imperial party drive up the resplendent, fairy-like, and unique avenue, Cecil followed the official.

He was guided along various passages and round unnumbered corners to the rear part of the colossal building. There, in a sumptuous bureau, the official introduced him to a still higher official, the Directeur, who had a decoration and a long, white moustache.

"Monsieur," said this latter, "I am desolated to have to inform you that the Minister of Fine Arts has withdrawn his original invitation for Box No. 74 to-night."

"I have received no intimation of the withdrawal," Cecil replied.

"No. Because the original invitation was not issued to you," said the Directeur, excited and nervous. "The Minister of Fine Arts instructs me to inform you that his invitation to meet the President and their Imperial Majesties cannot be bought and sold."

"But is it not notorious that many such invitations have been bought and sold?"

"It is, unfortunately, too notorious."

Here the Directeur looked at his watch and rang a bell impatiently.

"Then why am I singled out?"

The Directeur gazed blandly at Cecil. "The reason, perhaps, is best known to yourself," said he, and he rang the bell again.

"I appear to incommode you," Cecil remarked. "Permit me to retire."

"Not at all, I assure you," said the Directeur. "On the contrary. I am a little agitated on account of the non-arrival of Mademoiselle Malva."

A minor functionary entered.

"She has come?"

"No, Monsieur the Directeur."

"And it is nine-fifteen. *Sapristi!*"

The functionary departed.

"The invitation to Box No. 74," proceeded the Directeur, commanding himself, "was sold for two thousand francs. Allow me to hand you notes for the amount, dear monsieur."

"But I paid twenty-five thousand," said Cecil, smiling.

"It is conceivable. But the Minister can only concern himself with the original figure. You refuse the notes?"

"By no means," said Cecil, accepting them. "But I have brought here to-night three guests, including two ladies. Imagine my position."

"I imagine it," the Directeur responded. "But you will not deny that the Minister has always the right to cancel an invitation. Seats ought to be sold subject to the contingency of that right being exercised."

At that moment still another official plunged into the room.

"She is not here yet!" he sighed, as if in extremity.

"It is unfortunate," Cecil sympathetically put in.

"It is more than unfortunate, dear monsieur," said the Directeur, gesticulating. "It is unthinkable. The performance *must* begin at nine-thirty, and it *must* begin with the garden scene from 'Faust,' in which Mademoiselle Malva takes *Marguerite*."

"Why not change the order?" Cecil suggested.

"Impossible. There are only two other items. The first act of 'Lohengrin,' with Madame Félise, and the ballet 'Sylvia.' We cannot commence with the ballet. No one ever heard of such a thing. And do you suppose that Félise will sing before Malva? Not for millions. Not for a throne. The etiquette of sopranos is stricter than that of Courts. Besides, to-night we cannot have a German opera preceding a French one."

"Then the President and their Majesties will have to wait a little, till Malva arrives," Cecil said.

"Their Majesties wait! Impossible!"

"Impossible!" echoed the other official, aghast.

Two more officials entered. And the atmosphere of alarm, of being scotched, of being up a tree of incredible height, the atmosphere which at that moment permeated the whole of the vast region behind the scenes of the Paris Opéra, seemed to rush with them into the bureau of the Directeur and to concentrate itself there.

"Nine-twenty! And she couldn't dress in less than fifteen minutes."

"You have sent to the Hotel du Louvre?" the Directeur questioned despairingly.

"Yes, Monsieur the Directeur. She left there two hours ago."

Cecil coughed.

"I could have told you as much," he remarked, very distinctly

"What!" cried the Directeur. "You know Mademoiselle Malva?"

"She is among my intimate friends," said Cecil smoothly.

"Perhaps you know where she is?"

"I have a most accurate idea," said Cecil.

"Where?"

"I will tell you when I am seated in my box with my friends," Cecil answered.

"Dear monsieur," panted the Directeur, "tell us at once! I give you my word of honour that you shall have your box."

Cecil bowed.

"Certainly," he said. "I may remark that I had gathered information which led me to anticipate this difficulty with the Minister of Fine Arts—"

"But Malva, Malva—where is she?"

"Be at ease. It is only nine-twenty-three, and Mademoiselle Malva is less than three minutes away, and ready dressed. I was observing that I had gathered information which led me to anticipate this difficulty with the Minister of Fine Arts, and accordingly I took measures to protect myself. There is no such thing as absolute arbitrary power, dear Directeur, even in a Republic, and I have proved it. Mademoiselle Malva is in room No. 429 at the Grand Hotel, across the road. . . . Stay, she will not come without this note."

He handed out a small, folded letter from his waistcoat pocket.

Then he added: "Adieu, Monsieur the Directeur. You have just time to reach the State entrance in order to welcome the Presidential and Imperial party."

At nine-thirty, Cecil and his friends were ushered by a trinity of subservient officials into their box, which had been mysteriously emptied of its previous occupants. And at the same moment the monarchs, with monarchical punctuality, accompanied by the President, entered the Presidential box in the middle of the grand tier of the superb auditorium. The distinguished and dazzling audience rose to its feet, and the band played the National Anthem.

"You fixed it up then?" Belmont whispered under cover of the National Anthem. He was beaten, after all.

"Oh, yes!" said Cecil lightly. "A trivial misconception, nothing more. And I have made a little out of it, too."

"Indeed! Much?"

"No, not much! Two thousand francs. But you must remember that I have been less than half an hour in making them."

The curtain rose on the garden scene from "Faust."

IV

"My dear," said Eve.

When a woman has been definitely linked with a man, either by betrothal or by marriage, there are moments, especially at the commencement, when she assumes an air and a tone of absolute exclusive possession of him. It is a wonderful trick, which no male can successfully imitate, try how he will. One of these moments had arrived in the history of Eve Fincastle and her millionaire lover. They sat in a large, deserted public room, all gold, of the Grand Hotel. It was midnight less a quarter, and they had just returned, somewhat excited and flushed, from the glories of the gala performances. During the latter part of the evening, Eve had been absent from Cecil's box for nearly half an hour.

Kitty Sartorius and Lionel Belmont were conversing in an adjoining *salon*.

"Yes," said Cecil.

"Are you quite, quite sure that you love me?"

Only one answer is possible to such a question. Cecil gave it.

"That is all very well," Eve pursued with equal gravity and charm. "But it was really tremendously sudden, wasn't it? I can't think what you see in me, dearest."

"My dear Eve," Cecil observed, holding her hand, "the best things, the most enduring things, very often occur suddenly."

"Say you love me," she persisted.

So he said it, this time. Then her gravity deepened, though she smiled.

"You've given up all those—those schemes and things of yours, haven't you?" she questioned.

"Absolutely," he replied.

"My dear, I'm so glad. I never could understand why—"

"Listen," he said. "What was I to do? I was rich. I was bored. I had no great attainments. I was interested in life and in the arts, but not desperately, not vitally. You may, perhaps, say I should have taken up philanthropy. Well, I'm not built that way. I can't help it, but I'm not a born philanthropist, and the philanthropist without a gift for philanthropy usually does vastly more harm than good. I might have gone into business. Well, I should only have doubled my millions, while boring myself all the time. Yet the instinct which I inherited from my father, the great American instinct to be a little cleverer and smarter than someone else, drove me to action. It was part of my character, and one can't get away from one's character. So finally I took to these rather original 'schemes,' as you call them. They had the advantage of being exciting and sometimes dangerous, and though they were often profitable, they were not too profitable. In short, they amused me and gave me joy. They also gave me *you*."

Eve smiled again, but without committing herself.

"But you have abandoned them now completely?" she said.

"Oh, yes," he answered.

"Then what about this Opéra affair to-night?" She sprang the question on him sharply. She did her best to look severe, but the endeavour ended with a laugh.

"I meant to tell you," he said. "But how—how did you know? How did you guess?"

"You forget that I am still a journalist," she replied, "and still on the staff of my paper. I wished to interview Malva to-night for the *Journal*, and I did so. It was she who let out things. She thought I knew all about it; and when she saw that I didn't she stopped and advised me mysteriously to consult you for details."

"It was the scandal at the gala performance last autumn that gave me an action for making a corner in seats at the very next gala performance that should ever occur at the Paris Opéra," Cecil began his confession. "I knew that seats could be got direct from more or less minor officials at the Ministry of Fine Arts, and also that a large proportion of the people invited to these performances were prepared to sell their seats. You can't imagine how venal certain circles are in Paris. It just happened that the details and date of to-night's performance were announced on the day we arrived here. I could not resist the chance. Now you comprehend sundry strange absences of mine during the week. I went to a reporter on the *Echo de Paris* whom I knew, and who knows everybody. And we got out a list of the people likely to be invited and likely to be willing to sell their seats. We also opened negotiations at the Ministry."

"How on earth do these ideas occur to you?" asked Eve.

"How can I tell?" Cecil answered. "It is because they occur to me that I am I—you see. Well, in twenty-four hours my reporter and two of his friends had interviewed half the interviewable people in Paris, and the Minister of Fine Arts had sent out his invitations, and I had obtained the refusal of over three hundred seats, at a total cost of about seventy-five thousand francs. Then I saw that my friend the incomparable Malva was staying at the Ritz, and the keystone idea of the entire affair presented itself to me. I got her to offer to sing. Of course, her rival Félise could not be behind her in a patriotic desire to cement the friendliness of two great nations. The gala performance blossomed into a terrific boom. We took a kind of office in the Rue de la Paix. We advertised very discreetly. Every evening, after bidding you 'Good-night,' I saw my reporter and Lecky, and arranged the development of the campaign. In three days we had sold all our seats, except one box, which I kept, for something like two hundred thousand francs."

"Then this afternoon you merely bought the box from yourself?"

"Exactly, my love. I had meant the surprise of getting a box to come a little later than it did—say at dinner; but you and Belmont, between you, forced it on."

"And that is all?"

"Not quite. The minions of the Minister of Fine Arts were extremely cross. And they meant to revenge themselves on me by depriving me of my box at the last moment. However, I got wind of that, and by the simplest possible arrangement with Malva I protected myself. The scheme—my last bachelor fling, Eve—has been a great success, and the official world of Paris has been taught a lesson which may lead to excellent results."

"And you have cleared a hundred and twenty-five thousand francs?"

"By no means. The profits of these undertakings are the least part of them. The expenses are heavy. I reckon the expenses will be nearly forty thousand francs. Then I must give Malva a necklace, and that necklace must cost twenty-five thousand francs."

"That leaves sixty thousand clear?" said Eve.

"Say sixty-two thousand."

"Why?"

"I was forgetting an extra two thousand made this evening."

"And your other 'schemes'?" Eve continued her cross-examination. "How much have they yielded?"

"The Devonshire House scheme was a dead loss. My dear, why did you lead me to destroy that fifty thousand pounds? Waste not, want not. There may come a day when we shall need that fifty thousand pounds; and then—"

"Don't be funny," said Eve. "I am serious—very serious."

"Well, Ostend and Mr. Rainshore yielded twenty-one thousand pounds net. Bruges and the bracelet yielded nine thousand five hundred francs. Algiers and Biskra resulted in a loss of—"

"Never mind the losses," Eve interrupted. "Are there any more gains?"

"Yes, a few. At Rome last year I somehow managed to clear fifty thousand francs. Then there was an episode at the Chancellory at Berlin. And—"

"Tell me the total gains, my love," said Eve— "the gross gains."

Cecil consulted a pocket-book.

"A trifle," he answered. "Between thirty-eight and forty thousand pounds."

"My dear Cecil," the girl said, "call it forty thousand—a million francs—and give me a cheque. Do you mind?"

"I shall be charmed, my darling."

"And when we get to London," Eve finished, "I will hand it over to the hospitals anonymously."

He paused, gazed at her, and kissed her.

Then Kitty Sartorius entered, a marvellous vision, with Belmont in her wake. Kitty glanced hesitatingly at the massive and good-humoured Lionel.

"The fact is—" said Kitty, and paused.

"We are engaged," said Lionel. "You aren't surprised?"

"Our warmest congratulations!" Cecil observed. "No. We can't truthfully say that we are staggered. It is in the secret nature of things that a leading lady must marry her manager—a universal law that may not be transgressed."

"Moreover," said Eve later, in Cecil's private ear, as they were separating for the night, "we might have guessed much earlier. Theatrical managers don't go scattering five-hundred pound bracelets all over the place merely for business reasons."

"But he only scattered one, my dear," Cecil murmured.

"Yes, well. That's what I mean."

FURTHER ADVENTURES

Mr. Penfound's Two Burglars:
The Story of His Walk with Them

The chain of circumstances leading to the sudden and unexpected return of Mr. and Mrs. Penfound from their Continental holiday was in itself curious and even remarkable, but it has nothing to do with the present narrative, which begins with the actual arrival of Mr. and Mrs. Penfound before the portal of their suburban residence, No. 7, Munster Gardens, at a quarter before midnight on the 30th of August.

It was a detached house with a spacious triangular garden at the back; it had an air of comfort, of sobriety, of good form, of success; one divined by looking at it that the rent ran to about £80, and that the tenant was not a man who had to save up for quarter days. It was a credit to the street, which upon the whole, with its noble trees and its pretty curve, is distinctly the best street in Fulham. And, in fact, No. 7 in every way justified the innocent pride of the Penfounds.

"I can feel cobwebs all over me," said Mrs. Penfound, crossly, as they entered the porch and Mr. Penfound took out his latchkey. She was hungry, hot, and tired, and she exhibited a certain pettishness—a pettishness which Mr. Penfound, whenever it occurred, found a particular pleasure in soothing. Mr. Penfound himself was seldom ruffled.

Most men would have been preoccupied with the discomforts of the arrival, but not George Penfound. Mr. Penfound was not, and had never been, of those who go daily into the city by a particular train, and think the world is coming to an end if the newsagent fails to put the newspaper on the doorstep before 8 a.m.

Mr. Penfound had lived. He had lived adventurously and he had lived everywhere. He had slept under the stars and over the throbbing screws of ocean steamers. He knew the harbours of the British Empire, and the waste places of the unpeopled West, and the mysterious environs of foreign cities. He had been first mate of a tramp steamer, wood sawyer in Ontario, ganger on the Canadian Pacific Railway, clerk at a Rand mine, and land agent in California.

It was the last occupation that had happened to yield the eighty thousand dollars which rendered him independent and established him so splendidly, at the age of forty, in Fulham, the place of his birth. Thin, shrewd, clear, and kindly, his face was the face of a man who has learnt the true philosophy of life. He took the world as he found it, and he found it good.

To such a man an unexpected journey, even though it ended at a deserted and unprepared home, whose larder proved as empty as his stomach, was really nothing.

By the time Mr. Penfound had locked up the house, turned out the light in the hall, and arrived in the bedroom, Mrs. Penfound was fast asleep. He sat down in the armchair by the window, charmed by the gentle radiance of the night, and unwilling to go to bed. Like most men who have seen the world, he had developed the instincts of a poet, and was something of a dreamer. Half an hour—or it might have been an hour: poets are oblivious of time—had passed, when into Mr. Penfound's visions there entered a sinister element. He straightened himself stiffly in the chair and listened, smiling.

"By Jove!" he whispered. "I do believe it's a burglar. I'll give the beggar time to get fairly in, and then we'll have some fun."

It seemed to him that he heard a few clicking noises at the back of the house, and then a sound as if something was being shoved hard.

"The dining-room window," he said.

In a few minutes it became perfectly evident to his trained and acute ear that a burglar occupied the dining-room, and accordingly he proceeded to carry out other arrangements.

Removing his boots, he assumed a pair of soft, woollen house slippers which lay under the bed. Then he went to a chest of drawers, and took out two revolvers. Handling these lovingly, he glanced once at his sleeping wife, and, shod in the silent woollen, passed noiselessly out of the room. By stepping very close to the wall, so as to put as slight a strain as possible upon the woodwork, he contrived to descend to the half-landing without causing a sound, but on the half- landing itself there occurred an awful creak—a creak that seemed to reverberate into infinite space. Mr. Penfound stopped a second, but, perceiving the unwisdom of a halt, immediately proceeded.

In that second of consternation he had remembered that only two chambers of one revolver and one chamber of the other were loaded. It was an unfortunate mischance. Should he return and load fully? Preposterous! He remembered with pride the sensation which he had caused one night ten years before in a private shooting-saloon in Paris. Three shots to cripple one burglar—for *him*, it was a positive extravagance of means. And he continued down the stairs, cautiously but rapidly feeling his way.

The next occurrence brought him up standing at the dining-room door, which was open. He heard voices in the dining-room. There were, then, two burglars. Three shots for two burglars? Pooh! Ample! This was what he heard:—

"Did you drink out of this glass, Jack?"

"Not I. I took a pull out of the bottle."

"So did I."

"Well?"

There was a pause. Mr. Penfound discovered that by putting an eye to the crack at the hinges he could see the burglars, who had lighted one gas jet, and were sitting at the table. They were his first burglars, and they rather shocked his preconceived notions of the type. They hadn't the look of burglars—no bluish chins, no lowering eyes, no corduroy, no knotted red handkerchiefs.

One, the younger, dressed in blue serge, with linen collar and a soiled pink necktie, might have been a city clerk of the lower grade; he had light, bushy hair and a yellow moustache, his eyes were

large and pale blue, his chin weak; altogether Mr. Penfound decided that had he seen the young man elsewhere than in that
dining-room he would never have suspected him to be a burglar.
The other was of middle age, neatly dressed in dark grey, but with
a ruffian's face, and black hair, cut extremely close; he wore a soft
felt hat at a negligent poise, and was smoking a cigarette. He was
examining the glass out of which Mr. Penfound had but recently
drunk whisky.

"Look here, Jack," the man in grey said to his companion. "You
haven't drunk out of this glass, and I haven't; but someone's drunk
out of it. It's wet."

The young man paled, and with an oath snatched up the glass
to look at it. Mr. Penfound noticed how suddenly his features
writhed into a complicated expression of cowardice, cunning, and
vice. He no longer doubted that the youth was an authentic burglar. The older man remained calm.

"This house isn't so empty as we thought, my boy. There's someone here."

"Yes, gentlemen, there is," remarked Mr. Penfound, quietly
stepping into the room with a revolver upraised in each hand.

The young man dropped the glass, and, after rolling along the
table, it fell on the floor and broke, making a marvellous noise in
the silence.

"Well, I'm blowed!" exclaimed the burglar in grey, and turned
to the window.

"Don't stir; put your hands up, and look slippy—I mean business," said Mr. Penfound steadily.

The burglar in grey made two hasty steps to the window. Mr.
Penfound's revolver spoke—it was the one in his left hand, containing two shots—and with a muffled howl the burglar suddenly
halted, cursing with pain and anger.

"Hands up, both of you!" repeated Mr. Penfound imperturbably.

A few drops of blood appeared on the left wrist of the older
burglar, showing where he had been hit. With evident pain he
raised both hands to the level of his shoulders; the left hand clearly

was useless; it hung sideways in a peculiar fashion. The youthful criminal was trembling like a spray of maidenhair, and had his hands high up over his head.

Mr. Penfound joyfully reflected that no London burglar had ever before found himself in such a ridiculous position as these two, and he took a genuine, artistic pleasure in the spectacle.

But what to do next.

The youth began to speak with a whine like that of a beggar.

"Silence!" said Mr. Penfound impressively, and proceeded with his cogitations, a revolver firm and steady in each hand. The shot had evidently not wakened his wife, and to disturb her now from a refreshing and long-needed sleep in order to send her for the police would not only be unchivalrous, it would disclose a lack of resource, a certain clumsiness of management, in an affair which Mr. Penfound felt sure he ought to be able to carry neatly to an effective conclusion. Besides, if a revolver-shot in the house had not wakened his wife, what could wake her? He could not go up-stairs to her and leave the burglars to await his return.

Then an idea occurred to Mr. Penfound.

"Now, my men," he said cheerfully, "I think you understand that I am not joking, and that I can shoot a bit, and that, whatever the laws of this country, I *do* shoot." He waved the muzzle of one revolver in the direction of the grey man's injured wrist.

"Look here, governor," the owner of the wrist pleaded, "it hurts dreadful. I shall faint."

"Faint, then. I know it hurts."

The man's face was white with pain, but Mr. Penfound had seen too many strange sights in his life to be greatly moved by the sight of a rascal with a bullet in his anatomy.

"To proceed. You will stand side by side and turn round. The young gentleman will open the window, and you will pass out into the garden. March! Slower, slower, I say. Halt!"

The burglars were now outside, while Mr. Penfound was still within the room. He followed them, and in doing so stumbled over a black bag which lay on the floor. Fortunately he recovered himself instantly. He noticed lying on the top of the bag a small bunch of skeleton keys, some putty, and what looked like a thong of raw hide.

He also observed that three small panes of the French window had been forced inwards.

"Turn to your left, go down the pathway, and halt when you come to the side gate. And don't hurry, mind you."

They obeyed, without speaking even to each other. Mr. Penfound had no fear of their disobedience. He was within two yards of their heels, and he said to himself that his hands were superbly steady.

It was at this point that Mr. Penfound began to feel hungry, really hungry. The whisky had appeased the cravings of his stomach for a short time, but now its demands were imperious. Owing to the exigencies of the day's journey he had not had a satisfying meal for thirty hours; and Mr. Penfound since settling down had developed a liking for regular meals. However, there was nothing to be done at present.

He therefore proceeded with and safely accomplished his plan of driving the burglars before him into the street.

"Here," he thought, "we shall soon be seeing a policeman, or some late bird who will fetch a policeman." And he drove his curious team up Munster Park Gardens towards Fulham Road, that interminable highway, once rural but rural no longer.

The thoroughfares seemed to be absolutely deserted. Mr. Penfound could scarcely believe that London, even in the dead of night, could be so lonely. The gas-lamps shone steady in the still, warm air, and above them the star-studded sky, with a thin sickle moon, at which, however, beautiful as it was, Mr. Penfound could not look. His gaze was fixed on the burglars. As he inspected their backs he wondered what their thoughts were.

He felt that in their place he should have been somewhat amused by the humour of the predicament. But their backs showed no sign of feeling, unless it were that of resignation. The older man had dropped his injured arm, with Mr. Penfound's tacit consent, and it now hung loose by his side.

The procession moved slowly eastward along Fulham Road, the two burglars first, silent, glum, and disgusted, and Mr. Penfound with his revolvers close behind.

Still no policeman, no wayfarer. Mr. Penfound began to feel a little anxious. And his hunger was insufferable. This little procession of his could not move for ever. Something must occur, and Mr. Penfound said that something must occur quickly. He looked up at the houses with a swift glance, but these dark faces of brick, all with closed eyelids, gave him no sign of encouragement. He thought of firing his revolver in order to attract attention, but remembered in time that if he did so he would have only one shot left for his burglars, an insufficient allowance in case of contingencies.

But presently, as the clock of Fulham parish church struck three, Mr. Penfound beheld an oasis of waving palms and cool water in this desert; that is to say, he saw in the distance one of those coffee-stalls which just before midnight mysteriously dot themselves about London, only to disappear again at breakfast time. The burglars also saw it, and stopped almost involuntarily.

"Get on now," said Mr. Penfound gruffly, "and stop five paces *past* the coffee-stall. D'ye hear?"

"Yes, sir," whined the young burglar.

"Ay," remarked the old burglar coolly.

As Mr. Penfound approached the coffee-stall, he observed that it was no ordinary coffee-stall. It belonged to the aristocracy of coffee-stalls. It was painted a lovely deep crimson, and on this crimson, amid flowers and scrolls, had been inscribed the names of the delicacies within:—Tea, coffee, cocoa, rolls, sandwiches, toast, sausages, even bacon and eggs. Mr. Penfound's stomach called aloud within him at the rumour of these good things.

When the trio arrived, the stallkeeper happened to be bending over a tea-urn, and he did not notice the halt of the procession until Mr. Penfound spoke.

"I say," Mr. Penfound began, holding the revolvers about the level of his top waistcoat button, and with his eyes fixed on the burglars— "I say!"

"Tea or coffee?" asked the stallkeeper shortly, looking up.

"Neither—that is, at present," replied Mr. Penfound sweetly. "The fact is, I've got two burglars here."

"Two *what*—where?"

Mr. Penfound then explained the whole circumstances. "And I want you to fetch a couple of policemen."

The stallkeeper paused a moment. He was a grim fellow, so Mr. Penfound gathered from the corner of his eye.

"Well, that's about the best story as I ever 'eard," the stallkeeper said. "And you want me to fetch a policeman?"

"Yes; and I hope you'll hurry up. I'm tired of holding these revolvers."

"And I'm to leave my stall, am I?"

"Certainly."

The stallkeeper placed the first finger of his left hand upright against his nose.

"Well, I just ain't then. What d'ye take me for? A bloomin' owl? Look 'ere, mister: no kid! Nigh every night some jokers tries to get me away from my stall, so as they can empty it and run off. But I ain't been in this line nineteen year for nuthin'. No, you go and take yer tale and yer pistols and yer bloomin' burglars somewhere else. 'Ear?"

"As you please," said Mr. Penfound, with dignity. "Only I'll wait here till a policeman comes, or someone. You will then learn that I have told you the truth. How soon will a policeman be along?"

"Might be a 'our, might be more. There ain't likely to be no other people till four-thirty or thereabouts; that's when my trade begins."

Mr. Penfound was annoyed. His hunger, exasperated by the exquisite odours of the stall, increased every second, and the prospect of waiting an hour, even half an hour, was appalling.

Another idea occurred to him.

"Will you," he said to the stallkeeper, "kindly put one of those sausages into my mouth? I daren't loose these revolvers."

"Not till I sees yer money."

Hunger made Mr. Penfound humble, and he continued—

"Will you come round and take the money out of my pocket?"

"No, I won't. I don't leave this 'ere counter. I know yer dodges."

"Very well, I will wait."

"Steady on, governor. You aren't the only chap that's hungry."

Mr. Penfound turned sharply at the voice. It was the elder burglar who spoke, and the elder burglar had faced him and was approaching the stall, regardless of revolvers. Mr. Penfound noticed a twinkle in the man's eye, a faint appreciation of the fact that the situation was funny, and Mr. Penfound gave way to a slight smile. He was being disobeyed flatly, but for the life of him he could not shoot. Besides, there was no occasion to shoot, as the burglar was certainly making no attempt to escape. The fellow was brave enough, after all.

"Two slabs and a pint o' thick," he said to the stallkeeper, and was immediately served with a jug of coffee and two huge pieces of bread-and-butter, for which he flung down two-pence.

Mr. Penfound was astounded—he was too astounded to speak—by the coolness of this criminal.

"Look here," the elder burglar continued, quietly handing one of the pieces of bread-and-butter to his companion in sin, who by this time had also crept up, "you can put down them revolvers and tuck in till the peeler comes along. We know when we're copped, and we aren't going to skip. You tuck in, governor."

"Give it a name," said the stallkeeper, with an eye to business.

Mr. Penfound, scarcely knowing what he did or why he did it, put down one revolver and then the other, fished a shilling from his pocket, and presently was engaged in the consumption of a ham sandwich and coffee.

"You're a cool one," he said at length, rather admiringly, to the elder burglar.

"So are you," said the elder burglar; and he and Mr. Penfound both glanced somewhat scornfully at the other burglar, undersized, cringing, pale.

"Ever been caught before?" asked Mr. Penfound pleasantly.

"What's that got to do with you?"

The retort was gruff, final—a snub, and Mr. Penfound felt it as such. He had the curious sensation that he was in the presence of a superior spirit, a stronger personality than his own.

"Here's a policeman," remarked the stallkeeper casually, and they all listened, and heard the noise of regular footfalls away round a distant corner.

Mr. Penfound struggled inwardly with a sudden overmastering impulse, and then yielded.

"You can go," he said quietly to the elder burglar, "so clear off before the policeman sees you."

"Straight?" the man said, looking him in the eyes to make sure there was no joking.

"Straight, my friend. . . . Here, shake."

So it happened that Mr. Penfound and the elder burglar shook hands. The next instant Mr. Penfound was alone with the stall-keeper; the other two, with the celerity born of practice, had vanished into the night.

"Did you ever see such a man?" said Mr. Penfound to the stall-keeper, putting the revolvers in his pocket, and feeling strangely happy, as one who has done a good action.

"Yer don't kid me," was the curt reply. "It was all a plant. Want any think else? Because if not, ye'd best go."

"Yes, I do," said Mr. Penfound, for he had thought of his wife. He spent seven-pence in various good things, and was just gathering his purchases together when the policeman appeared.

"Good night, officer," he called out blithely, and set off to run home, as though for his life.

As he re-entered the bedroom at No. 7 his wife sat up in bed, a beautiful but accusing figure.

"George," she said, "where have you been?"

"My love," he answered, "I've been out into the night to get you this sausage, and this cake, and this sandwich. Eat them. They will do you good."

MIDNIGHT AT THE GRAND BABYLON

I

Well, said the doctor, you say I've been very secretive lately.
Perhaps I have. However, I don't mind telling you—just you fellows—the whole history of the affair that has preoccupied me. I
shan't assert that it's the most curious case in all my experience.
My experience has been pretty varied, and pretty lively, as you
know, and cases are curious in such different ways. Still, a poisoning business is always a bit curious, and this one was extremely
so. It isn't often that a person who means to commit murder by
poison calls in a physician to assist him and deliberately uses the
unconscious medico as his tool. Yet that is exactly what happened.
It isn't often that a poisoner contrives to hit on a poison which is
at once original, almost untraceable, and to be obtained from any
chemist without a doctor's prescription. Yet that, too, is exactly
what happened. I can assure you that the entire episode was a lesson to me. It opened my eyes to the possibilities which lie ready to
the hand of a really intelligent murderer in this twentieth century.
People talk about the masterpieces of poisoning in the middle ages.
Pooh! Second-rate! They didn't know enough in the middle ages
to achieve anything which a modern poisoner with genius would
deem first-rate; they simply didn't know enough. Another point in
the matter which forcibly struck me was the singular usefulness of
a big London hotel to a talented criminal. You can do precisely
what you please in a big hotel, and nobody takes the least notice.
You wander in, you wander out, and who cares? You are only an

item in a crowd. And when you have reached the upper corridors you are as lost to pursuit and observation as a needle in a hay-stack. You may take two rooms, one after the other, in different names, and in different parts of the hotel; the servants and officials will be none the wiser, because the second floor knows not the third, nor the third the fourth; you may oscillate between those two rooms in a manner to puzzle Inspector Anderson himself. And you are just as secure in your apartments as a mediaeval baron in his castle—yes, and more! On that night there were over a thousand guests in the Grand Babylon Hotel (there was a ball in the Gold Rooms, and a couple of banquets); and in the midst of all that diverse humanity, unperceived, unsuspected, a poignant and terrible drama was going on, and things sc occurred that I tumbled right into it. Well, I'll tell you.

II

I was called in to the Grand Babylon about nine p.m.; suite No. 63, second floor, name of Russell. The outer door of the suite was opened for me by a well-dressed woman of thirty or so, slim, with a face expressive and intelligent rather than handsome. I liked her face—I was attracted by its look of honesty and alert good-nature.

"Good evening, doctor," she said. She had a charming low voice, as she led me into a highly-luxurious drawing-room. "My name is Russell, and I wish you to see a young friend of mine who is not well." She hesitated and turned to an old bald-headed man, who stood looking out of the window at the twilight panorama of the Thames. "My friend's solicitor, Mr. Dancer," she explained. We bowed, Mr. Dancer and I.

"Nothing serious, I hope," I remarked.

"No, no!" said Miss Russell.

Nevertheless, she seemed to me to be extremely nervous and anxious, as she preceded me into the bedroom, a chamber quite as magnificent as the drawing-room.

On the bed lay a beautiful young girl. Yes, you may laugh, you fellows, but she was genuinely beautiful. She smiled faintly as we

entered. Her features had an ashy tint, and tiny drops of cold per-
spiration stood on the forehead. However, she certainly wasn't very
ill—I could see that in a moment, and I fixed my conversational
tone accordingly.

"Do you feel as if you could breathe freely, but that if you did it
would kill you?" I inquired, after I had examined her. And she nodded, smiling again. Miss Russell also smiled, evidently pleased that
I had diagnosed the case so quickly.

My patient was suffering from a mild attack of pseudo-angina,
nothing worse. Not angina pectoris, you know—that's usually as-
sociated with old age. Pseudo-angina is a different thing. With a
weak heart, it may be caused by indigestion. The symptoms are
cardiac spasms, acute pain in the chest, a strong disinclination to
make even the smallest movement, and a state of mental depression, together with that queer fancy about breathing. The girl had
these symptoms, and she also had a headache and a dicrotism of
the pulse—two pulsations instead of one, not unusual. I found that
she had been eating a too hearty dinner, and that she had suffered
from several similar attacks in the immediate past.

"You had a doctor in before?" I asked.

"Yes," said Miss Russell. "But he was unable to come to-night,
and as your house is so near we sent for you."

"There is no danger whatever—no real cause for anxiety," I
summed up. "I will have some medicine made up instantly."

"Trinitrin?" demanded Miss Russell.

"Yes," I answered, a little astonished at this readiness. "Your
regular physician prescribed it?"

(I should explain to you that trinitrin is nothing but nitro-glycerine in a non-explosive form.)

"I think it was trinitrin," Miss Russell replied, with an appearance of doubtfulness. "Perhaps you will write the prescription and
I will despatch a messenger at once. I should be obliged, doctor, if
you would remain with us until—if you would remain with us."

"Decidedly!" I said. "I will remain with pleasure. But do accept
my assurance," I added, gazing at her face, so anxious and appre-
hensive, "that there is no cause for alarm."

She smiled and concurred. But I could see that I had not convinced her. And I began to suspect that she was not after all so intelligent as I had imagined. My patient, who was not now in any pain, lay calmly, with closed eyes.

III

Do not forget the old bald-headed lawyer in the drawing-room.

"I suppose you are often summoned to the Grand Babylon, sir, living, as you do, just round the corner," he remarked to me somewhat pompously. He had a big nose and a habit of staring at you over his eye-glasses with his mouth wide-open, after having spoken. We were alone together in the drawing-room. I was waiting for the arrival of the medicine, and he was waiting for—I didn't know what he was waiting for.

"Occasionally. Not often," I responded. "I am called more frequently to the Majestic, over the way."

"Ah, just so, just so," he murmured.

I could see that he meant to be polite in his high and dry antique legal style; and I could see also that he was very bored in that hotel drawing-room. So I proceeded to explain the case to him, and to question him discreetly about my patient and Miss Russell.

"You are, of course, aware, sir, that the young lady is Miss Spanton, Miss Adelaide Spanton?" he said.

"What? Not 'the' Spanton?"

"Precisely, sir. The daughter of Edgar Spanton, my late client, the great newspaper proprietor."

"And this Miss Russell?"

"Miss Russell was formerly Miss Adelaide's governess. She is now her friend, and profoundly attached to the young lady; a disinterested attachment, so far as I can judge, though naturally many people will think otherwise. Miss Adelaide is of a very shy and retiring disposition; she has no other friends, and she has no near relatives. Save for Miss Russell she is, sir, if I may so phrase it, alone in the world."

"But Miss Spanton is surely very wealthy?"

"You come to the point, sir. If my young client reaches her twenty-first birthday she will be the absolute mistress of the whole of her father's fortune. You may have noticed in the public press that I swore his estate at more than three millions."

"And how far is Miss Spanton from her twenty-first birthday?" I demanded.

The old lawyer glanced at his watch.

"Something less than three hours. At midnight she will have legally entered on her 22nd year."

"I see," I said. "Now I can understand Miss Russell's anxiety, which refuses to be relieved even by my positive assurance. No doubt Miss Russell has worked herself up into a highly nervous condition. And may I inquire what will happen—I mean, what would have happened, if Miss Spanton had not reached her majority?"

"The entire estate would have passed to a cousin, a Mr. Samuel Grist, of Melbourne. I daresay you know the name. Mr. Grist is understood to be the leading theatrical manager in Australia. Speaking as one professional man to another, sir, I may venture to remark that Mr. Grist's reputation is more than a little doubtful—you may have heard—many transactions and adventures. Ha, ha! Still, he is my late client's sole surviving relative, except Miss Adelaide. I have never had the pleasure of meeting him; he confines himself exclusively to Australia."

"This night then," I laughed, "will see the end of any hopes which Mr. Grist may have entertained."

"Exactly, sir," the lawyer agreed. "It will also see the end of Miss Russell's immediate anxieties. Upon my word, since Mr. Spanton's regrettable death, she has been both father and mother to my lonely young client. A practical woman, sir, Miss Russell! And the excessiveness of her apprehensions, if I may so phrase it, must be excused. She has begged me to remain here till midnight, in order that I may witness to Miss Spanton's—er—vitality, and also in order to obtain Miss Spanton's signature to certain necessary documents. I should not be surprised, sir, if she requested you also to remain. She is not a woman to omit precautions."

"I'm afraid I can't stop till twelve," I said. The conversation ceased, and I fell into meditation.

I do not mind admitting that I was deeply impressed by what I will call the romantic quality of the situation. I thought of old Spanton, who had begun with something less than nothing and died virtually the owner of three daily papers and twenty-five weeklies and monthlies. I thought of Spantons, Ltd., and their colossal offices spreading half round Salisbury Square. Why, I even had a copy of the extra special edition of the *Evening Gazette* in my pocket! Do any of you fellows remember Spanton starting the *Evening Gazette*? He sold three hundred thousand the first day. And now old Spanton was dead—you know he died of drink, and there was nothing left of the Spanton blood except this girl lying there on the bed, and the man in Australia. And all the Spanton editors, and the Spanton sub-editors, and the Spanton artists, and the Spanton reporters and compositors, and the Spanton rotary presses, and the Spanton paper mills, and the Spanton cyclists, were slaving and toiling to put eighty thousand a year into this girl's purse. And there she was, feeble and depressed, and solitary, except for Miss Russell, and the man in Australia perhaps hoping she would die; and there was Miss Russell, worrying and fussing and apprehending and fearing. And the entire hotel oblivious of the romantic, I could almost say the pathetic, situation. And then I thought of Miss Spanton's future, burdened with those three millions, and I wondered if those three millions would buy her happiness.

"Here is the medicine, doctor," said Miss Russell, entering the drawing-room hurriedly, and handing me the bottle with the chemist's label on it. I went with her into the bedroom. The beautiful Adelaide Spanton was already better, and she admitted as much when I administered the medicine—two minims of a one per cent, solution of trinitrin, otherwise nitro-glycerine, the usual remedy for pseudo-angina.

Miss Russell took the bottle from my hand, corked it and placed it on the dressing-table. Shortly afterwards I left the hotel. The lawyer had been right in supposing that Miss Russell would ask me to stay, but I was unable to do so. I promised, however, to return in an hour, all the while insisting that there was not the slightest danger for the patient.

                                    IV

It was 10.30 when I came back.

"Second floor!" I said carelessly to the lift-boy, and he whirled me upwards; the Grand Babylon lifts travel very fast.

"Here you are, sir," he murmured respectfully, and I stepped out.

"Is this the second floor?" I asked suddenly.

"Beg pardon! I thought you said seventh, sir."

"It's time you were in bed, my lad!" was my retort, and I was just re-entering the lift when I caught sight of Miss Russell in the corridor. I called to her, thinking she would perhaps descend with me, but she did not hear, and so I followed her down the corridor, wondering what was her business on the seventh floor. She opened a door and disappeared into a room.

"Well?" I heard a sinister voice exclaim within the room, and then the door was pushed to; it was not latched.

"I did say the seventh!" I called to the lift-boy, and he vanished with his machine.

The voice within the room startled me. It gave me furiously to think, as the French say. With a sort of instinctive unpremeditated action I pressed gently against the door till it stood ajar about an inch. And I listened.

"It's a confounded mysterious case to me!" the voice was saying, "that that dose the other day didn't finish her. We're running it a dashed sight too close! Here, take this—it's all ready, label and everything. Substitute the bottles. I'll run no risks this time. One dose will do the trick inside half an hour, and on that I'll bet my boots!"

"Very well," said Miss Russell, quite calmly. "It's pure trinitrin, is it?"

"You're the coolest customer that I ever struck!" the voice exclaimed, in an admiring tone. "Yes, it's pure trinitrin—beautiful, convenient stuff! Looks like water, no taste, very little smell, and so volatile that all the doctors on the Medical Council couldn't trace it at a post-mortem. Besides the doctor prescribed a solution of trinitrin, and you got it from the chemist, and in case there's a rumpus we can shove the mistake on to the chemist's dispenser, and a fine old row he'll get into. By the way, what's the new doctor like?"

"Oh! So-so!" said Miss Russell, in her even tones.

"It's a good thing on the whole, perhaps, that I arranged that carriage accident for the first one!" the hard, sinister voice remarked. "One never knows. Get along now at once, and don't look so anxious. Your face belies your voice. Give us a kiss!"

"To-morrow!" said Miss Russell.

I hurried away, as it were drunk, overwhelmed with horror and amazement, and turning a corner so as to avoid discovery, reached the second floor by the staircase. I did not wish to meet Miss Russell in the lift.

My first thought was not one of alarm for Adelaide Spanton—of course, I knew I could prevent the murder—but of profound sorrow that Miss Russell should have proved to be a woman so unspeakably wicked. I swore never to trust a woman's face again. I had liked her face. Then I dwelt on the chance, the mere chance, my careless pronunciation, a lift-boy's error, which had saved the life of the poor millionaire girl. And lastly I marvelled at the combined simplicity and ingenuity of the plot. The scoundrel upstairs—possibly Samuel Grist himself—had taken the cleverest advantage of Miss Spanton's tendency to pseudo-angina. What could be more clever than to poison with the physician's own medicine? Very probably the girl's present attack had been induced by an artful appeal to her appetite; young women afflicted as she was are frequently just a little greedy. And I perceived that the villain was correct in assuming that nitro-glycerine would never be traced at a post-mortem save in the smallest possible quantity—just such a quantity as I had myself prescribed. He was also right in his assumption that the pure drug would infallibly kill in half an hour.

I pulled myself together, and having surreptitiously watched Miss Russell into Suite No. 63, I followed her. When I arrived at the bedroom she was pouring medicine from a bottle; a maid stood at the foot of the bed.

"I am just giving the second dose," said Miss Russell easily to me.

"What a nerve!" I said to myself, and aloud: "By all means!"

She measured the dose, and approached the bed without a tremor. Adelaide Spanton opened her mouth.

"Stop!" I cried firmly. "We'll delay that dose for half an hour. Kindly give me the glass!" I took the glass from Miss Russell's passive fingers. "And I would like to have a word with you now, Miss Russell!" I added.

The maid went swiftly from the room.

V

The old bald-headed lawyer had gone down to the hotel smoking-saloon for a little diversion, and we faced each other in the drawing-room—Miss Russell and I. The glass was still in my hand.

"And the new doctor is so-so, eh?" I remarked.

"What do you mean?" she faltered.

"I think you know what I mean," I retorted. "I need only tell you that by a sheer chance I stumbled upon your atrocious plot—the plot of that scoundrel upstairs. All you had to do was to exchange the bottles, and administer pure trinitrin instead of my prescribed solution of it, and Miss Spanton would be dead in half an hour. The three millions would go to the Australian cousin, and you would doubtless have your reward—say, a cool hundred thousand, or perhaps marriage. And you were about to give the poison when I stopped you."

"I was not!" she cried. And she fell into a chair, and hid her face in her hands, and then looked, as it were longingly, towards the bed-room.

"Miss Spanton is in no danger," I said sneeringly. "She will be quite well to-morrow. So you were not going to give the poison, after all?" I laughed.

"I beg you to listen, doctor," she said at length, standing up. "I am in a most invidious position. Nevertheless, I think I can convince you that your suspicions against me are unfounded."

I laughed again. But secretly I admired her for acting the part so well.

"Doubtless!" I interjected sarcastically, in the pause.

"The man upstairs is Samuel Grist, supposed to be in Australia. It is four months ago since I, who am Adelaide Spanton's sole friend, discovered that he was scheming her death. The skill of his methods appalled me. There was nothing to put before the police, and yet I had a horrible fear of the worst. I felt that he would stop at nothing—absolutely at nothing. I felt that, if we ran away, he would follow us. I had a presentiment that he would infallibly succeed, and I was haunted by it day and night. Then an idea occurred to me—I would pretend to be his accomplice. And I saw suddenly that that was the surest way—the sole way, of defeating him. I approached him and he accepted the bait. I carried out all his instructions, except the fatal instructions. It is by his orders, and for his purposes, that we are staying in this hotel. Heavens! To make certain of saving my darling Adelaide, I have even gone through the farce of promising to marry him!"

"And do you seriously expect me to believe this?" I asked coldly.

"Should I have had the solicitor here?" she demanded, "if I had really meant—meant to—"

She sobbed momentarily, and then regained control of herself.

"I don't know," I said, "but it occurs to me that the brain that was capable of deliberately arranging a murder to take place in the presence of the doctor might have some hidden purpose in securing also the presence of the solicitor at the performance."

"Mr. Grist is unaware that the solicitor is here. He has been informed that Mr. Dancer is my uncle, and favourable to the—to the—" she stopped, apparently overcome.

"Oh, indeed!" I ejaculated, adding: "And after all you did not mean to administer this poison! I suppose you meant to withdraw the glass at the last instant?"

"It is not poison," she replied.

"Not poison?"

"No. I did not exchange the bottles. I only pretended to."

"There seems to have been a good deal of pretending," I observed. "By the way, may I ask why you were giving this stuff, whether it is poison or not, to my patient? I do not recollect that I ordered a second dose."

"For the same reason that I pretended to change the bottle. For the benefit of the maid whom we saw just now in the bedroom."

"And why for the benefit of the maid?"

"Because I found out this morning that she is in the pay of Grist. That discovery accounts for my nervousness to-night about Adelaide. By this time the maid has probably told Mr. Grist what has taken place, and, and—I shall rely on your help if anything should happen, doctor. Surely, surely, you believe me?"

"I regret to say, madam," I answered, "that I find myself unable to believe you at present. But there is a simple way of giving credence to your story. You state that you did not exchange the bottles. This liquid, then, is the medicine prescribed by me, and it is harmless. Oblige me by drinking it."

And I held the glass towards her.

She took it.

"Fool!" I said to myself, as soon as her fingers had grasped it. "She will drop it on the floor, and an invaluable piece of evidence will be destroyed."

But she did not drop it on the floor. She drank it at one gulp, and looked me in the eyes, and murmured, "Now do you believe me?"

"Yes," I said. And I did.

At the same moment her face changed colour, and she sank to the ground. "What have I drunk?" she moaned. The glass rolled on the carpet, unbroken.

Miss Russell had in fact drunk a full dose of pure trinitrin. I recognised all the symptoms at once. I rang for assistance. I got a stomach pump. I got ice, and sent for ergot and for atropine. I injected six minims of the *Injectis Ergotini Hypodermica*. I despaired of saving her; but I saved her, after four injections. I need not describe to you all the details. Let it suffice that she recovered.

"Then you did exchange the bottles?" I could not help putting this question to her as soon as she was in a fit state to hear it.

"I swear to you that I had not meant to," she whispered. "In my nervousness I must have confused them. You have saved Adelaide's life."

"I have saved yours, anyway," I said.

"But you believe me?"

"Yes," I said; and the curious thing is that I did believe her. I was convinced, and I am convinced, that she did not mean to exchange the bottles.

"Listen!" she exclaimed. We could hear Big Ben striking twelve.

"Midnight," I said.

She clutched my hand with a swift movement. "Go and see that my Adelaide lives," she cried almost hysterically.

I opened the door between the two rooms and went into the sleeping chamber.

"Miss Spanton is dozing quietly," I said, on my return.

"Thank God!" Miss Russell murmured. And then old bald-headed Mr. Dancer came into the room, blandly unconscious of all that had passed during his sojourn in the smoking saloon.

When I left the precincts of the Grand Babylon at one o'clock, the guests were beginning to leave the Gold Rooms, and the great courtyard was a scene of flashing lights, and champing horses, and pretty laughing women.

"What a queer place a hotel is!" I thought.

Neither Mr. Grist nor the mysterious maid was seen again in London. Possibly they consoled each other. The beautiful Adelaide Spanton—under my care, ahem!—is completely restored to health.

Yes, I am going to marry her. No, not the beautiful Adelaide, you duffers—besides she is too young for my middle age—but Miss Russell. Her Christian name is Ethel. Do you not like it? As for the beautiful Adelaide, there is now a viscount in the case.

The Police Station

Lord Trent has several times remarked to me that I am a philosopher. And I am one. I have guided my life by four rules: To keep my place, to make others keep theirs, to save half my income, and to beware of women. The strict observance of these rules has made me (in my station) a successful and respected man. Once, and only once, I was lax in my observance, and that single laxity resulted in a most curious and annoying adventure, which I will relate.

It was the fourth rule that I transgressed. I did not beware of a woman. The woman was Miss Susan Berry, lady's maid to the Marchioness of Cockfosters.

The Cockfosters family is a very old one. To my mind its traditions are superior to anything in the peerage of Great Britain; but then I may be prejudiced. I was brought up in the Cockfosters household, first at Cockfosters Castle in Devon, and afterwards at the well-known town house at the south-east corner of Eaton Square.

My father was valet to the old Marquis for thirty years; my mother rose from the position of fifth housemaid to be housekeeper at the Castle. Without ever having been definitely assigned to the situation, I became, as it were by gradual attachment, valet to Lord Trent—eldest son of the Marquis, and as gay and good-natured a gentleman as ever drank brandy-and-soda before breakfast.

When Lord Trent married Miss Edna Stuyvesant, the American heiress, and with some of her money bought and furnished in a superb manner a mansion near the northwest corner of Eaton

Square, I quite naturally followed him across the Square, and soon found myself, after his lordship and my lady, the most considerable personage at No. 441. Even the butler had to mind his "p's" and "q's" with me.

Perhaps it was this pre-eminence of mine which led to my being selected for a duty which I never cared for, and which ultimately I asked his lord- ship to allow me to relinquish—of course he did so. That duty related to the celebrated Cockfosters emeralds. Lady Trent had money (over a million sterling, as his lordship himself told me), but money could not buy the Cockfosters emeralds, and having seen these she desired nothing less fine. With her ladyship, to desire was to obtain. I have always admired her for that trait in her character. Being an American she had faults, but she knew her own mind, which is a great thing; and I must admit that, on the whole, she carried herself well and committed few blunders. She must have been accustomed to good servants.

In the matter of the emeralds, I certainly took her side. Strictly speaking, they belonged to the old Marchioness, but the Marchioness never went into society; she was always engaged with temperance propaganda, militant Protestantism, and that sort of thing, and consequently never wore the emeralds. There was no valid reason, there- fore, why Lady Trent should not have the gratification of wearing them. But the Marchioness, I say it with respect, was a woman of peculiar and decided views. She had, in fact, fads; and one of her fads was the emeralds. She could not bear to part with them. She said she was afraid something might happen to the precious heirlooms.

A prolonged war ensued between the Marchioness and my lady, and ultimately a compromise was effected. My lady won permission to wear the emeralds whenever she chose, but they were always to be brought to her and taken back again by Susan Berry, in whom the Marchioness had more confidence than in anyone else in the world. Consequently, whenever my lady required the emeralds, word was sent across the Square in the afternoon; Susan Berry brought them over, and Susan Berry removed them at night when my lady returned from her ball or reception.

The arrangement was highly inconvenient for Susan Berry, for sometimes it would be very late when my lady came home; but the Marchioness insisted, and since Susan Berry was one of those persons who seem to take a positive joy in martyrising themselves, she had none of my pity. The nuisance was that someone from our house had to accompany her across the Square. Eaton Square is very large (probably the largest in London, but I may be mistaken on such a trivial point); its main avenue is shut in by trees; and at 2 a.m. it is distinctly not the place for an unprotected female in charge of valuable property. Now the Marchioness had been good enough to suggest that she would prefer me to escort her maid on this brief nocturnal journey. I accepted the responsibility, but I did not hide my dislike for it. Knowing something of Miss Berry's disposition, I knew that our household would inevitably begin, sooner or later, to couple our names together, and I was not deceived.

Such was the situation when one night—it was a Whit-Monday, I remember, and about a quarter past one—Lord and Lady Trent returned from an entertainment at a well-known mansion near St. James's Palace. I got his lordship some whisky in the library, and he then told me that I might go to bed, as he should not retire for an hour or so. I withdrew to the little office off the hall, and engaged in conversation with the second footman, who was on duty. Presently his lordship came down into the hall and began to pace about—it was a strange habit of his—smoking a cigarette. He caught sight of me.

"Saunders," he said, "I told you you could go to bed."

"Yes, my lord."

"Why don't you go?"

"Your lordship forgets the emeralds."

"Ah, yes, of course." He laughed. I motioned to the footman to clear out.

"You don't seem to care for that job, Saunders," his lordship resumed, quizzing me. "Surely Berry is a charming companion. In your place I should regard it as excellent fun. But I have often told you that you have no sense of humour."

"Not all men laugh at the same jokes, my lord," I observed.

As a matter of fact, in earlier and wilder days, his lordship had sometimes thrown a book or a boot at me for smiling too openly in the wrong place.

The conversation might have continued further, for his lordship would often talk with me, but at that moment Susan Berry appeared with the bag containing the case in which were the emeralds.

Lady Trent's own maid was with her, and the two stood talking for an instant at the foot of the stairs, while Lady Trent's maid locked the bag and handed the key to Berry. Heaven knows how long that simple business would have occupied had not the voice of my lady resounded from the first floor, somewhat excitedly calling for her maid, who vanished with a hurried good-night. His lordship had already departed from the hall.

"May I relieve you of the bag, Miss Berry?" I asked.

"Thank you, Mr. Saunders," she replied, "but the Marchioness prefers that I myself should carry it."

That little dialogue passed between us every time the emeralds had to be returned.

We started on our short walk, Miss Berry and I, proceeding towards the main avenue which runs through the centre of the Square east and west. It was a beautiful moonlight night. Talking of moonlight nights, I may as well make my confession at once. The fact is that Miss Berry had indeed a certain influence over me. In her presence I was always conscious of feeling a pleasurable elation—an excitement, a perturbation, which another man might have guessed to be the beginning of love.

I, however, knew that it was not love. It was merely a fancy. It only affected me when I was in her company. When she was absent I could regard her in my mind's eye as she actually was— namely, a somewhat designing young woman, with dark eyes and too much will of her own. Nevertheless, she had, as I say, a certain influence over me, and I have already remarked that it was a moonlight night.

Need I say more? In spite of what I had implied to Lord Trent I did enjoy the walk with Susan Berry. Susan Berry took care that I should. She laid herself out to fascinate me; turning her brunette face up to mine with an air of deference, and flashing upon me the glance of those dark lustrous eyes.

She started by sympathising with me in the matter of the butler. This was, I now recognise, very clever of her, for the butler has always been a sore point with me. I began to think (be good enough to remember the moonlight and the trees) that life with Susan Berry might have its advantages.

Then she turned to the topic of her invalid sister, Jane Mary, who was lame and lived in lodgings near Sloane Street, and kept herself, with a little aid from Susan, by manufacturing artificial flowers. For a month past Miss Berry had referred regularly to this sister, who appeared to be the apple of her eye. I had no objection to the topic, though it did not specially interest me; but on the previous evening Miss Berry had told me, with a peculiar emphasis, that her poor dear sister often expressed a longing to see the famous Cockfosters emeralds, and that she resided quite close too. I did not like that.

To-night Miss Berry made a proposition which alarmed me. "Mr. Saunders," she said insinuatingly, "you are so good-natured that I have almost a mind to ask you a favour. Would you object to walking round with me to my sister's—it is only a few minutes away—so that I could just give her a peep at these emeralds. She is dying to see them, and I'm sure the Marchioness wouldn't object. We should not be a quarter of an hour away."

My discretion was aroused. I ought to have given a decided negative at once; but somehow I couldn't, while Susan was looking at me.

"But surely your sister will be in bed," I suggested.

"Oh, no," with a sigh. "She has to work very late—very late indeed. And besides, if she is, I could take them up to her room. It would do her good to see them, and she has few pleasures."

"The Marchioness might not like it," I said, driven back to the second line of fortification. "You know your mistress is very particular about these emeralds."

"The Marchioness need never know," Susan Berry whispered, putting her face close up to mine. "No one need know, except just us two."

The accent which she put on those three words "just us two," was extremely tender.

I hesitated. We were already at the end of the Square, and should have turned down to the left towards Cockfosters House.

"Come along," she entreated, placing her hand on my shoulder.

"Well, you know—" I muttered, but I went along with her towards Sloane Street. We passed Eaton Place.

"Really, Miss Berry—" I began again, collecting my courage.

Then there was a step behind us, and another hand was placed on my shoulder. I turned round sharply. It was a policeman. His buttons shone in the moonlight.

"Your name is Charles Saunders," he said to me; "and yours Susan Berry," to my companion.

"True," I replied, for both of us.

"I have a warrant for your arrest!"

"Our arrest?"

"Yes, on a charge of attempting to steal some emeralds, the property of the Marquis of Cockfosters."

"Impossible," I exclaimed.

"Yes," he sneered, "that's what they all say."

"But the emeralds are here in this bag."

"I know they are," he said. "I've just copped you in time. But you've been suspected for days."

"The thing is ridiculous," I said, striving to keep calm. "We are taking the emeralds back to Lady Cockfosters, and—"

Then I stopped. If we were merely taking the emeralds back to Lady Cockfosters, that is, from one house in Eaton Square to another house in Eaton Square, what were we doing out of the Square?

I glanced at Susan Berry. She was as white as a sheet. The solution of the puzzle occurred to me at once. Susan's sister was an ingenious fiction. Susan was a jewel thief, working with a gang of jewel thieves, and her request that I would accompany her to this mythical sister was part of a plan for stealing the emeralds.

"At whose instance has the warrant been issued?" I asked.

"The Marquis of Cockfosters."

My suspicions were only too well confirmed.

I did not speak a word to Susan Berry. I could not. I merely looked at her.

"You'll come quietly to the station?" the policeman said.

"Certainly," I replied. "As for us, the matter can soon be cleared up. I am Lord Trent's valet, No. 441, Eaton Square, and he must be sent for."

"Oh, must he!" the constable jeered. "Come on. Perhaps you'd prefer a cab."

A four-wheeler was passing. I myself hailed the sleepy cabman, and we all three got in. The policeman prudently took the bag from Susan's nerveless hands. None of us spoke. I was too depressed, Susan was probably too ashamed, and the constable was no doubt too bored.

After a brief drive we drew up. Another policeman opened the door of the cab, and over the open portal of the building in front of us I saw the familiar blue lamp, with the legend "Metropolitan Police" in white letters. The two policemen carefully watched us as we alighted, and escorted us up the steps into the station. Happily, there was no one about; my humiliation was abject enough without that.

Charles Saunders a prisoner in a police station! I could scarcely credit my senses. One becomes used to a police station—in the newspapers; but to be inside one—that is different, widely different.

The two policemen took us into a bare room, innocent of any furniture save a wooden form, a desk, a chair, some printed notices of rewards offered, and an array of handcuffs and revolvers on the mantelpiece. In the chair, with a big book in front of him on the desk, sat the inspector in charge. He was in his shirt-sleeves.

"A hot night," he said, smiling, to the policeman.

I silently agreed.

It appeared that we were expected.

They took our full names, our addresses and occupations, and then the inspector read the warrant to us. Of course, it didn't explain things in the least. I began to speak.

"Let me warn you," said the inspector, "that anything you say now may be used against you at your trial."

My trial!

"Can I write a note to Lord Trent?" I asked, nettled.

"Yes, if you will pay for a cab to take it."

I threw down half-a-crown, and scribbled a line to my master, begging him to come at once.

"The constable must search you," the inspector said, when this was done and the first policeman had disappeared with the note.

"I will save him the trouble," I said proudly, and I emptied my pockets of a gold watch and chain, a handkerchief, two sovereigns, a sixpence, two halfpennies, a bunch of keys, my master's linen book, and a new necktie which I had bought that very evening; of which articles the inspector made an inventory.

"Which is the key of the bag?" asked the inspector. The bag was on the desk in front of him, and he had been trying to open it.

"I know nothing of that," I said.

"Now you, Susan Berry, give up the key," the inspector said, sternly, turning to her.

For answer Susan burst into sobs, and flung herself against my breast. The situation was excessively embarrassing for me. Heaven knows I had sufficient reason to hate the woman, but though a thief, she was in distress, and I must own that I felt for her.

The constable stepped towards Susan.

"Surely," I said, "you have a female searcher?"

"A female searcher! Ah, yes!" smiled the inspector, suddenly suave. "Is she here, constable?"

"Not now, sir; she's gone."

"That must wait, then. Take them to the cells."

"Sorry, sir, all the cells are full. Bank Holiday drunks."

The inspector thought a moment.

"Lock 'em up in the back room," he said. "That'll do for the present. Perhaps the male prisoner may be getting an answer to his note soon. After that they'll have to go to Vine Street or Marlborough."

The constable touched his helmet, and marched us out. In another moment we were ensconced in a small room, absolutely bare of any furniture, except a short wooden form. The constable was locking the door when Susan Berry screamed out: "You aren't going to lock us up here together in the dark?"

"Why, what do you want? Didn't you hear the cells are full?"

I was profoundly thankful they were full. I did not fancy a night in a cell.

"I want a candle," she said, fiercely.

He brought one, or rather half of one, stuck in a bottle, and placed it on the mantelpiece. Then he left us.

Again I say the situation was excessively embarrassing. For myself, I said nothing. Susan Berry dropped on the form, and hiding her face in her hands, gave way to tears without any manner of restraint. I pitied her a little, but that influence which previously she had exercised over me was gone. "Oh, Mr. Saunders," she sobbed, "what shall we do?" And as she spoke she suddenly looked up at me with a glance of feminine appeal. I withstood it.

"Miss Berry," I said severely, "I wonder that you can look me in the face. I trusted you as a woman, and you have outraged that trust. I never dreamed that you were—that you were an adventuress. It was certainly a clever plot, and but for the smartness of the police I should, in my innocence, have fallen a victim to your designs. For myself, I am grateful to the police. I can understand and excuse their mistake in regarding me as your accomplice. That will soon be set right, for Lord Trent will be here. In the meantime, of course, I have been put to considerable humiliation. Nevertheless, even this is better than having followed you to your sister's. In your 'sister's' lodging I might have been knocked senseless, or even murdered. Moreover, the emeralds are safe."

She put on an innocent expression, playing the injured maiden.

"Mr. Saunders, you surely do not imagine—"

"Miss Berry, no protestations, I beg. Let me say now that I have always detected in your character something underhand, something crafty."

"I swear—" she began again.

"Don't trouble," I interrupted her icily, "for I shall not believe you. This night will certainly be a warning to me."

With that I leaned my back against the mantelpiece, and abandoned myself to gloomy thought. It was a moment for me of self-abasement. I searched my heart, and I sorrowfully admitted that my predicament was primarily due to disobeying that golden rule—beware of women. I saw now that it was only my absurd fancy for this wicked creature which had led me to accept the office of guarding those emeralds during their night-passage across Eaton Square. I ought to have refused in the first place, for the job was entirely outside my functions; strictly, the butler should have done it.

And this woman in front of me—this Susan Berry, in whom the old Marchioness had such unbounded trust! So she belonged to the confraternity of jewel thieves—a genus of which I had often read, but which I had never before met with. What audacity such people must need in order to execute their schemes!

But then the game was high. The Cockfosters emeralds were worth, at a moderate estimate, twelve thousand pounds. There are emeralds and emeralds, the value depends on the colour; these were the finest Colombian stones, of a marvellous tint, and many of them were absolutely without a flaw. There were five stones of seven carats each, and these alone must have been worth at least six thousand pounds. Yes, it would have been a great haul, a colossal haul.

Time passed, the candle was burning low, and there was no sign of Lord Trent. I went to the door and knocked, first gently, then more loudly, but I could get no answer. Then I walked about the room, keeping an eye on Susan Berry, who had, I freely admit, the decency to avoid my gaze. I was beginning to get extremely tired. I wished to sit down, but there was only one form; Susan Berry was already upon it, and, as I said before, it was a very short form. At last I could hold out no longer. Taking my courage in both hands, I sat down boldly at one end of the form. It was a relief to me. Miss Berry sighed. There were not six inches between us.

The candle was low in the socket, we both watched it. Without a second's warning the flame leapt up and then expired. We were in the dark. Miss Berry screamed, and afterwards I heard her cry-ing. I myself made no sign. Fortunately the dawn broke almost immediately.

By this time I was getting seriously annoyed with Lord. Trent. I had served him faithfully, and yet at the moment of my genuine need he had not come to my succour. I went again to the door and knocked with my knuckles. No answer. Then I kicked it. No answer. Then I seized the handle and violently shook it. To my astonish-ment the door opened. The policeman had forgotten to lock it.

I crept out into the passage, softly closing the door behind me. It was now quite light. The door leading to the street was open, and I could see neither constables nor inspector. I went into the charge room; it was empty. Then I proceeded into the street. On the pavement a piece of paper was lying. I picked it up; it was the note which I had written to Lord Trent.

A workman happened to be loitering along a road which crossed this street at right angles. I called out and ran to him.

"Can you tell me," I asked, "why all the officers have left the police station?"

"Look 'ere, matey." he says, "you get on 'ome; you've been making a night of it, that's wot you 'ave."

"But, seriously," I said.

Then I saw a policeman at a distant corner. The workman whistled, and the policeman was obliging enough to come to us.

"'Ere's a cove wants to know why all the police 'as left the po-lice station," the workman said.

"What police station?" the constable said sharply.

"Why, this one down here in this side-street," I said, pointing to the building. As I looked at it I saw that the lamp which I had observed on the previous night no longer hung over the doorway.

The constable laughed good-humouredly.

"Get away home," he said.

I began to tell him my story.

"Get away home," he repeated—gruffly this time, "or I'll run you in."

"All right." I said huffily, and I made as if to walk down the other road. The constable and the workman grinned to each other and departed. As soon as they were out of sight, I returned to my police station.

It was not a police station! It was merely a rather large and plain-fronted empty house, which had been transformed into a police station, for one night only, by means of a lamp, a desk, two forms, a few handcuffs, and some unparalleled cheek. Jewel thieves they were, but Susan Berry was not among them. After all Susan Berry probably had an invalid sister named Jane Mary.

The first policeman, the cabman, the second policeman, the inspector—these were the jewel thieves, and Susan Berry and I (and of course the Marchioness) had been the victims of as audacious and brilliant a robbery as was ever planned. We had been robbed openly, quietly, deliberately, with the aid of a sham police station. Our movements must have been watched for weeks. I gave my meed of admiration to the imagination, the skill, and the sangfroid which must have gone to the carrying out of this coup.

Going back into the room where Susan Berry and I had spent the night hours, I found that wronged woman sweetly asleep on the form, with her back against the wall. I dared not wake her. And so I left her for the present to enjoy some much-needed repose. I directed my steps in search of Eaton Square, having closed the great door of my police station.

At length I found my whereabouts, and I arrived at No. 441 at five o'clock precisely. The morning was lovely. After some trouble I roused a housemaid, who let me in. She seemed surprised, but I ignored her. I went straight upstairs and knocked at my master's door. To wake him had always been a difficult matter, and this morning the task seemed more difficult than ever. At last he replied sleepily to my summons.

"It is I—Saunders—your lordship."

"Go to the devil, then."

"I must see your lordship instantly. Very seriously."

"Eh, what? I'll come in a minute," and I heard him stirring, and the voice of Lady Trent.

How should I break the news to him? What would the Marchioness say when she knew? Twelve thousand pounds' worth of jewels is no trifle. Not to mention my gold watch, my two sovereigns, my sixpence, and my two halfpennies. And also the half-crown which I had given to have the message despatched to his lordship. It was the half-crown that specially rankled.

Lord Trent appeared at the door of his room, arrayed in his crimson dressing-gown.

"Well, Saunders, what in the name of—"

"My lord," I stammered, and then I told him the whole story.

He smiled, he laughed, he roared.

"I daresay it sounds very funny, my lord," I said, "but it wasn't funny at the time, and Lady Cockfosters won't think it very funny."

"Oh, won't she! She will. No one will enjoy it more. She might have taken it seriously if the emeralds had been in the bag, but they weren't."

"Not in the bag, my lord!"

"No. Lady Trent's maid ran off with the bag, thinking that your mistress had put the jewels in it. But she had not. Lady Trent came to the top of the stairs to call her back, as soon as she found the bag gone, but you and Berry were out of the house. So the emeralds stayed here for one night. They are on Lady Trent's dressing-table at the present moment. Go and get a stiff whisky, Saunders. You need it. And then may I suggest that you should return for the sleeping Berry? By the way, the least you can do is to marry her, Saunders."

"Never, my lord!" I said with decision. "I have meddled sufficiently with women."

The Adventure of the Prima Donna

Many years ago the fear of dynamite stalked through the land. An immense organisation of anarchists whose headquarters were in the United States had arranged for a number of simultaneous displays in London, Glasgow, and Quebec. As is well known now, the Parliament House at Quebec and the gasworks at Glasgow were to be blown up, while the programme for London included Scotland Yard, most of Whitehall, the House of Commons, the Tower, and four great railway stations thrown in.

This plot was laid bare, stopped, and made public, and—except a number of people who happened quite innocently to carry black bags—no one was put to the slightest inconvenience.

The dynamite scare was deemed to be at an end. But the dread organisation was in fact still active, as the sixty policemen who were injured in what is called the "Haymarket Massacre" explosion at Chicago, on May 4, 1886, have dire occasion to know.

Everyone who reads the papers is familiar with the details of the Haymarket Massacre. Few people, however, are aware that a far more dastardly outrage had been planned, to intimidate London a few days later. Through the agency of a courageous woman this affair too was unmasked in its turn, but for commercial and other reasons it was kept from the general public.

The scheme was to blow up the Opera House at Co vent Garden on the first night of the season. Had the facts got abroad, the audience would probably have been somewhat sparse on that occasion; but the facts did not get abroad, and the house was crowded in

140

every part; for the famous *prima donna* Louise Vesea (since retired) was singing "Marguerite," in "Faust," and enthusiasm about her was such that though the popular tenor had unaccountably thrown up his engagement, the price of stalls rose to thirty-three shillings. The police were sure of themselves, and the evening passed off with nothing more explosive than applause. Nevertheless, that night, after the curtain had fallen and Louise Vesea had gathered up all the wreaths and other tributes of admiration which had been showered upon her, there happened the singular incident which it is our purpose to record.

Vesea, wrapped in rich furs—it was midnight, and our usual wintry May—was just leaving the stage door for her carriage, when a gentleman respectfully accosted her. He was an English detective on special service, and Vesea appeared to know him.

"It will be desirable for you to run no risks, Madame," he said. "So far as we know all the principals have left the country in alarm, but there are always others."

Vesea smiled. She was then over thirty, in the full flower of her fame and beauty. Tall, dark, calm, mysterious, she had the firm yet gentle look of one who keeps a kind heart under the regal manner induced by universal adoration.

"What have I to fear?" she said.

"Vengeance," the detective answered simply. "I have arranged to have you shadowed, in case—"

"You will do nothing of the kind," she said. "The idea is intolerable to me. I am not afraid."

The detective argued, but in vain.

"It shall be as you wish, Madame," he said, ultimately.

Vesea got into her carriage, and was driven away. The pair of chestnuts travelled at a brisk trot through the dark deserted streets of Soho towards the West End. The carriage had crossed Regent Street and was just entering Berkeley Square when a hansom, coming at a gallop along Struton Street on the wrong side of the road, collided violently with Vesea's horses at the corner.

At the same moment another carriage, a brougham, came up and stopped. A gentleman jumped out, and assisted in disengaging

Vesea's coachman and footman from the medley of harness and horse-flesh. This done, he spoke to Vesea, who, uninjured, was standing on the footpath.

"One of your chestnuts will have to be shot," he said, raising his hat. "May I place my own carriage at your disposal?"

Vesea thankfully accepted his offer.

"Where to?" he inquired.

"Upper Brook Street," she answered. "But you are sure I do not inconvenience you?"

"Curiously enough," he said, "I live in Upper Brook Street myself, and if I may accompany you—"

"You are more than kind," she said, and they both entered the brougham, the gentleman having first thoughtfully taken the number of the peccant cabby, and given some valuable advice to Vesea's coachman.

The brougham disappeared at a terrific pace. But it never went within half a mile of Upper Brook Street. It turned abruptly to the north, crossed Oxford Street, and stopped in front of a large house in a remote street near Paddington Station. At the same instant the door of the house opened, and a man ran down to the carriage. In a moment Vesea, with a cloth wrapped round her head, was carried struggling into the house, and the brougham departed. The thing was done as quickly and silently as in a dream.

The cloth was removed at length, and Vesea found herself in a long bare room, furnished only with chairs and a table. She realised that the carriage accident was merely part of a plot to capture her without fuss and violence. She was incapable of fear, but she was extremely annoyed and indignant. She looked round for the man who enticed her into his brougham. He was not to be seen; his share of the matter was over. Two other men sat at the table. Vesea stared at them in speechless anger. As to them, they seemed to ignore her.

"Where is the Chief?" said one to the other.

"He will be here in three minutes. We are to proceed with the examination; time is short."

Then the two men turned to Vesea, and the elder spoke.

"You will be anxious to know why you are here," he said.

She gazed at him scornfully, and he continued:

"You are here because you have betrayed the anarchist cause."

"I am not an anarchist," she said coldly.

"Admitted. But a week ago a member of our society gave you a warning to keep away from the Opera House to-night. In so warning you he was false to his oath."

"Do you refer to Salti, the tenor?" she asked.

"I do. You perceive we have adherents in high places. Salti, then, warned you—and you instantly told the police. That was your idea of gratitude. Did Salti love you?"

"I decline to be cross-examined."

"It is immaterial. We know that he loved you. Now it is perilous for an anarchist to love."

"I do not believe that Salti is one of you," she broke in.

"He is not," the man said quietly. "He is dead. He was in the way."

In spite of herself she started, and both men smiled cynically.

"The point is this," the elder man proceeded. "We do not know how much Salti told you. It is possible that he may have blurted out other and more important—er—schemes than this of the Opera House which has failed. Have you anything to say?"

"Nothing," she answered.

"Ah! We expected that. Now, let me point out that you are dangerous to us, that there is only one possible course open to you. You must join us."

"Join you?" she exclaimed, and then laughed.

"Yes," the man said. "I repeat there is no alternative—none whatever. You must take the oaths."

"And if I refuse?"

The man shrugged his shoulders, and after a suggestive pause murmured:

"Well— think of Salti."

"I do refuse," she said.

A door opened at the other end of the room, and a third man entered.

"The Chief!" said the younger of the men at the table. "He will continue the examination."

The newcomer was comparatively youthful—under thirty—and had the look of a well-born Italian. He gave a glance at Vesea, stood still, and then approached the table and sat down.

"This is Louise Vesea," the first speaker said, and rapidly indicated how far he had gone. There was a long silence.

"Thanks, brothers," the Chief said. "By a strange coincidence I know this lady—this woman, and I feel convinced that it will be better, in the interests of our cause, if—if I examine her alone." He spoke with authority, and yet with a certain queer hesitation.

The two men silently, but with obvious reluctance, rose and left the room.

When they were alone, the great singer and the Chief fronted each other in silence.

"Well?" said Vesea.

"Madame," the Chief began slowly and thoughtfully. "Do you remember singing in Milan ten years ago? You were at the beginning of your career then, but already famous."

His voice was rich and curiously persuasive.

Without wishing to do so, Vesea nodded an affirmative.

"One night you were driving home from the opera, and there was a riot going on in the streets. The police were everywhere. People whispered of a secret revolutionary society among the students of the University. As for the students, after a pitched battle near the Cathedral, they were flying. Suddenly, looking from your carriage, you saw a very youthful student, who had been struck on the head, fall down in the gutter and then get up again and struggle on. You stopped your carriage. 'Save me,' the youth cried, 'Save me, Signorina. If the police catch me I shall get ten years' imprisonment!' You opened the door of your carriage, and the youth jumped in. 'Quick, under the rug,' you said quietly. You did not ask me any questions. You didn't stay to consider whether the youth might be a dangerous person. You merely said, 'Quick, under the rug!' The youth crept under the rug. The carriage moved on slowly, and the police, who shortly appeared, never thought of looking within it for a fugitive young anarchist. The youth was saved. For two days you had him in your lodging, and then he got safely away to the coast, and so by ship to another country. Do you remember that incident, Madame?"

"I remember it well," she answered. "What happened to the youth?"

"I am he," the Chief said.

"You?" she exclaimed. "I should scarcely have guessed but for your voice. You are changed."

"In our profession one changes quickly."

"Why do you remind me of that incident?" she asked.

"You saved my life then. I shall save yours now."

"Is my life really in danger?"

"Unless you joined us—yes."

She laughed incredulously.

"In London! Impossible!"

He made a gesture with his hands.

"Do not let us argue on that point," he said gravely. "Go through that door," he pointed to the door by which he himself had entered. "You will find yourself in a small garden. The garden gate leads to a narrow passage past some stables and so into the street. Go quickly, and take a cab. Don't return to your own house. Go some-where else—anywhere else: And leave London early to-morrow morning."

He silently opened the door for her.

"Thank you," she said. His seriousness had affected her. "How shall you explain my departure to your—your friends?"

"In my own way," he replied calmly. "When a man has deliber-ately betrayed his cause, there is only one explanation."

"Betrayed his cause!" She repeated the phrase wonderingly.

"Madame," he said, "do you suppose they will call it anything else? Go at once. I will wait half an hour before summoning my comrades. By that time they will have become impatient. Then you will be safe, and I will give them my explanation."

"And that will be?"

He put her right hand to his lip and then stopped.

"Good-bye, Madame," he said without replying to the question. "We are quits. I kiss your hand."

Almost reluctantly Louise Vesea went forth. And as she reached the street she felt for the first time that it was indeed a fatal danger from which she had escaped. She reflected that the Chief had imposed no secrecy upon her, made no conditions; and she could not help but admire such a method of repaying a debt. She wondered what his explanation to his comrades would be.

Half an hour later, when Vesea was far away, there was the sound of a revolver shot. The other two plotters rushed into the room which the *prima donna* had left, and found all the explanation which the Chief had vouchsafed.

The Episode in Room 222

The date was the fifth of November, a date easy to remember; not that I could ever fail to recall it, even without the aid of the associations which cluster round Guy Fawkes. It was a Friday—and yet there are people who affect to believe that Friday is not a day singled out from its six companions for mystery, strangeness, and disaster! The number of the room was 222, as easy to remember as the date; not that I could ever fail to recall the number also. Every circumstance in the affair is fixed in my mind immovably and for ever. The hotel I shall call by the name of the Grand Junction Terminus Hotel. If this tale were not a simple and undecorated record of fact, I might with impunity choose for its scene any one of the big London hotels in order by such a detail to give a semblance of veracity to my invention; but the story happens to be absolutely true, and I must therefore, for obvious reasons, disguise the identity of the place where it occurred. I would only say that the Grand Junction Railway is one of the largest and one of the best-managed systems in England, or in the world; and that these qualities of vastness and of good management extend also to its immense Terminus Hotel in the North of Central London. The caravanserai (I have observed that professional writers invariably refer to a hotel as a caravanserai) is full every night in the week except Friday, Saturday, and Sunday; and every commercial traveller knows that, except on these nights, if he wishes to secure a room at the Grand Junction he must write or telegraph for it in advance. And there are four hundred bedrooms.

147

It was somewhat late in the evening when I arrived in London. I had meant to sleep at a large new hotel in the Strand, but I felt tired, and I suddenly, on the spur of the moment, decided to stay at the Grand Junction, if there was space for me. It is thus that Fate works.

I walked into the hall, followed by a platform porter with my bag. The place seemed just as usual, the perfection of the commonplace, the business-like, and the unspiritual.

"Have you a room?" I asked the young lady in black, whose yellow hair shone gaily at the office window under the electric light.

She glanced at her ledgers in the impassive and detached manner which hotel young ladies with yellow hair invariably affect, and ejaculated:

"No. 221."

"Pity you couldn't make it all twos," I ventured, with timid jocularity. (How could I guess the import of what I was saying?)

She smiled very slightly, with a distant condescension. It is astonishing the skill with which a feminine hotel clerk can make a masculine guest feel small and self-conscious.

"Name?" she demanded.

"Edge."

"Fourth floor," she said, writing out the room-ticket and handing it to me.

In another moment I was in the lift.

No. 221 was the last door but one at the end of the eastern corridor of the fourth floor. It proved to be a double-bedded room, large, exquisitely ugly, but perfectly appointed in all matters of comfort; in short, it was characteristic of the hotel. I knew that every bedroom in that corridor, and every bedroom in every corridor, presented exactly the same aspect. One instinctively felt the impossibility of anything weird, anything bizarre, anything terrible, entering the precincts of an abode so solid, cheerful, orderly, and middle-class. And yet—but I shall come to that presently.

It will be well for me to relate all that I did that evening. I washed, and then took some valuables out of my bag and put them in my pocket. Then I glanced round the chamber, and amongst other satisfactory details noticed that the electric lights were so fixed that I could read in bed without distressing my eyes. I then went downstairs, by the lift, and into the smoke-room. I had dined on board the express, and so I ordered nothing but a cafe noir and a packet of Virginian cigarettes. After finishing the coffee I passed into the billiard-room, and played a hundred up with the marker. To show that my nerves were at least as steady as usual that night, I may mention that, although the marker gave me fifty and beat me, I made a break of twenty odd which won his generous approval. The game concluded, I went into the hall and asked the porter if there were any telegrams for me. There were not. I noticed that the porter—it was the night-porter, and he had just come on duty—seemed to have a peculiarly honest and attractive face. Wishing him good-night, I retired to bed. It was something after eleven. I read a chapter of Mr. Walter Crane's "The Bases of Design," and having turned off the light, sank into the righteous slumber of a man who has made a pretty break of 20 odd and drunk nothing but coffee. At three o'clock I awoke—not with a start, but rather gradually. I know it was exactly three o'clock because the striking of a notoriously noisy church clock in the neighbourhood was the first thing I heard. But the clock had not wakened me. I felt sure that something else, something far more sinister than a church clock, had been the origin of disturbance.

I listened. Then I heard it again—It. It was the sound of a groan in the next room.

"Someone indisposed, either in body or mind," I thought lightly, and I tried to go to sleep again. But I could not sleep. The groans continued, and grew more poignant, more fearsome. At last I jumped out of bed and turned on the light—I felt easier when I had turned on the light.

"That man, whoever he is, is dying." The idea, as it were, sprang at my throat. "He is dying. Only a dying man, only a man who saw Death by his side and trembled before the apparition, could groan like that."

I put on some clothes, and went into the corridor. The corridor seemed to stretch away into illimitable distance; and far off, miles off, a solitary electric light glimmered. My end of the corridor was a haunt of gloomy shadows, except where the open door allowed the light from my bedroom to illuminate the long monotonous pattern of the carpet. I proceeded to the door next my own—the door of No. 222, and put my ear against the panel. The sound of groans was now much more distinct and more terrifying. Yes. I admit that I was frightened. I called. No answer.

"What's the matter?" I inquired. No answer. "Are you ill, or are you doing this for your own amusement?" It was with a sort of bravado that I threw this last query at the unknown occupant of the room. No answer. Then I tried to open the door, but it was fast.

"Yes," I said to myself; "either he's dying or he's committed a murder and is feeling sorry for it. I must fetch the night-porter."

Now, hotel lifts are not in the habit of working at three a.m., and so I was compelled to find my way along endless corridors and down flights of stairs apparently innumerable. Here and there an electric light sought with its yellow eye to pierce the gloom. At length I reached the hall, and I well recollect that the tiled floor struck cold into my slippered but sockless feet.

"There's a man either dying or very ill in No. 222," I said to the night-porter. He was reading *The Evening News*, and appeared to be very snug in his basket chair.

"Is that so, sir?" he replied.

"Yes," I insisted. "I think he's dying. Hadn't you better do something?"

"I'll come upstairs with you," he answered readily, and without further parley we began the ascent. At the first floor landing the night-porter stopped and faced me. He was a man about forty-five—every hall-porter seems to be that age—and he looked like the father of a family.

"If you think he's dying, sir, I'll call up the manager, Mr. Thorn."

"Do," I said.

The manager slept on the first floor, and he soon appeared—a youngish man in a terra-cotta Jaeger dressing-gown, his eyes full of sleep, yet alert and anxious to do his duty. I had seen him previously in the billiard-room. We all three continued our progress to the fourth floor. Arrived in front of No. 222 we listened intently, but we could only hear a faint occasional groan.

"He's nearly dead," I said. The manager called aloud, but there was no answer. Then he vainly tried to open the door. The night-porter departed, and returned with a stout pair of steel tongs. With these, and the natural ingenuity peculiar to hotel-porters, he forced open the door, and we entered No. 222.

A stout, middle-aged man lay on the bed fully dressed in black. On the floor near the bed was a silk hat. As we approached the great body seemed to flutter, and then it lay profoundly and terribly still. The manager put his hand on the man's head, and held the glass of his watch to the man's parted grey lips.

"He is dead," said the manager.

"H'm!" I said.

"I'm sorry you've been put to any inconvenience," said the manager, "and I'm much obliged to you."

The cold but polite tone was a request to me to re-enter my own chamber, and leave the corpse to the manager and the night-porter. I obeyed.

"What about that man?" I asked the hall-porter early the next, or rather the same, morning. I had not slept a wink since three o'clock, nor had I heard a sound in the corridor.

"What man, sir?" the porter said.

"You know," I returned, rather angrily. "The man who died in the night—No. 222."

"I assure you, sir," he said, "I haven't the least notion what you mean."

Yet his face seemed as honest and open as ever.

I inquired at the office for the manager, and after some difficulty saw him in his private room.

"I thought I'd just see about that man," I began.

"What man?" the manager asked, exactly as the porter had asked.

"Look here," I said, as I was now really annoyed, "it's all very well giving instructions to the hall-porter, and I can quite understand you want the thing kept as quiet as possible. Of course I know that hotels have a violent objection to corpses. But as I saw the corpse, and was of some assistance to you—"

"Excuse me," said the manager. "Either you or I must be completely mad. And," he added, "I don't think it is myself."

"Do you mean to say," I remarked with frosty sarcasm, "that you didn't enter Room 222 with me this morning at three a.m. and find a dead man there?"

"I mean to say just that," he answered.

"Well." I got no further. I paid my bill and left. But before leaving, I went and carefully examined the door of No. 222. The door plainly showed marks of some iron instrument.

"Here," I said to the porter as I departed. "Accept this half-crown from me. I admire you."

I had a serious illness extending over three months. I was frequently delirious, and nearly every day I saw the scene in Room No. 222. In the course of my subsequent travels, I once more found myself, late one night, at the Grand Junction Terminus Hotel.

"Mr. Edge," said the night-porter, "I've been looking out for you for weeks and weeks. The manager's compliments, and he would like to see you in his room."

Again I saw the youngish, alert manager.

"Mr. Edge," he began at once, "it is probable that I owe you an apology. At any rate, I think it right to inform you that on the night of the fifth of November, the year before last, exactly twelve months before your last visit here, a stout man died in Room No. 222, at three a.m. I forgot the circumstance when you last came to see me in this room."

"It seems queer," I said coldly, "that you should have forgotten such a circumstance."

"The fact is," he replied, "I was not the manager at that time. My predecessor died two days after the discovery of the corpse in Room 222."

"And the night-porter—is he, too, a new man?"

"Yes," said the manager. "The porter who, with the late manager, found the corpse in Room 222, is now in Hanwell Lunatic Asylum."

I paused, perhaps in awe.

"Then you think," I said, "that I was the victim of a hallucination on my previous visit here? You think I had a glimpse of the world of spirits?"

"On these matters," said the manager, "I prefer to think nothing."

Saturday to Monday

So at length I yielded to repeated invitations, and made up my mind to visit the Vernons again. And it was in June. I had not been for nearly two years. The last visit was in the month of August: I remembered it too well—that year, that month, that day!

Under the most favourable circumstances, it needs enterprise and energy for a Londoner to pay a weekend visit to a friend's house in the country. No matter how intimate the friend—and the Vernons, though charming and full of good nature, were not really very intimate friends of mine—there is always an element of risk in the affair; I will go further and say an element of preliminary unpleasantness. It means the disarrangement of regular habits; it means packing one's bag and lugging it into a hansom; it means a train-journey; it often means a drive at the other end; it means sleeping in a strange bed and finding a suitable hook for one's razor strop the next morning; it means accommodating oneself to a new social atmosphere, and the expenditure of much formal politeness. And suppose some hitch occurs—some trifling contretemps to ruffle the smoothness of the hours—where are you then? You are bound to sit tight and smile till Monday, and at parting to enlarge on your sorrow that the visit is over, all the while feeling intensely relieved; and you have got nothing in exchange for your discomfort and inconvenience save the satisfaction of duty done— a poor return, I venture to add. You know you have wasted a weekend, an irrecoverable weekend of eternity.

However, I boarded the train at St. Pancras in a fairly cheerful mood, and I tried to look on the bright side of life. The afternoon was certainly beautiful, and the train not too crowded, and I derived some pleasure, too, from the contemplation of a new pair of American boots which I had recently purchased. I remembered that Mrs. Vernon used to accuse me of a slight foppishness in the matter of boots, at the same time wishing audibly (in his hearing) that Jack would give a little more attention to the lower portions of his toilet; Jack was a sportsman, and her husband. And I thought of their roomy and comfortable house on the side of the long slope to Bedbury, and of their orchard and the hammocks under the trees in the orchard, and of tea and cakes being brought out to those hammocks, and of the sunsets over the Delectable Mountains (we always called them the Delectable Mountains because they are the identical hills which Bunyan had in mind when he wrote "The Pilgrim's Progress"), and of Jack's easy drawl and Mrs. Vernon's chatter, and the barking of the dogs, and the stamping of the horses in the stable. And I actually thought: This will be a pleasant change after London.

"I do hope they won't be awkward and self-conscious," I said to myself. "And I also must try not to be."

You see I was thinking of that last visit and what occurred during it. I was engaged to be married then, to a girl named Lucy Wren. Just as I had arrived at the Vernons' house in their dog-cart the highly rural postman came up in his cart, and after delivering some letters produced still another letter and asked if anyone of the name of Bostock was staying there. I took the letter: the address was in Lucy's handwriting (I had seen her only on the previous night, and of course she knew of my visit). I read the letter, standing there in the garden near the front door, and having read it I laughed loudly and handed it to Mrs. Vernon, saying: "What do you think of that for a letter?" In the letter Lucy said that she had decided to jilt me (she didn't use those words—oh no!), and that on the following day she was going to be married to another man. Yes, that was a cheerful visit I paid to the Vernons, that August! At first I didn't know what I was doing. They soothed me, calmed me.

They did their best. It wasn't their fault after all. They suggested I should run back to town and see Lucy; Jack offered to go with me. (Jack!) I declined. I declined to do anything. I ate hearty meals. I insisted on our usual excursions. I talked a lot. I forced them to pretend that nothing had happened. And on Monday morning I went off with a cold smile. But it was awful. It stood between me and the Vernons for a long time, a terrible memory. And when next Mrs. Vernon encountered me, in London, there were tears in her eyes and she was speechless.

Now you will understand better why I said to myself, with much sincerity: "I do hope they won't be awkward and self-conscious. And I also must try not to be."

As the train approached Bedbury I had qualms. I had qualms about the advisability of this visit to the Vernons. How could it possibly succeed, with that memory stalking like a ghost in the garden near the front door of their delightful and hospitable house? How could? Then we rumbled over the familiar bridge, and I saw the familiar station yard, and the familiar dog-cart, and the familiar Dalmatian dog, and the familiar white mare that was rather young and skittish when Lucy jilted me. "That mare must be rising seven now," I thought, "and settled down in life."

I descried Mrs. Vernon waiting on the platform to welcome me, with the twins. Alas! I had forgotten the twins, those charming and frail little girls always dressed alike. Invariably, on my previous visits, I had brought something for the twins—a toy, a box of sweets, a couple of bead necklaces. Never once had I omitted to lay my tribute on the altar of their adorable infancy. And now I had forgotten, and my forgetfulness saddened me, because I knew that it would sadden them; they would expect, and they would be disappointed; they would taste the bitterness of life. "My poor little dears!" I thought, as they smiled and shouted, to see my head out of the carriage window, "I feel for you deeply."

This beginning was a bad one. Like all men who have suffered without having deserved to suffer, I was superstitious, and I felt that the beginning augured ill. I resigned myself, even before the train had quite stopped, to a constrained and bored weekend with the Vernons.

"Well?" I exclaimed, with an affectation of jollity, descending from the carriage.

"Well?" responded Mrs. Vernon, with the same affectation.

It was lamentable, simply lamentable, the way in which that tragic memory stood between us and prevented either of us from showing a true, natural, simple self to the other. Mrs. Vernon could say little; I could say little; and what we did say was said stiffly, clumsily. Perhaps it was fortunate, on the whole, that the twins were present. They at any rate were natural and self-possessed.

"And how old are you now?" I asked them.

"We are seven," they answered politely in their high, thin voices.

"Then you are like the little girl's family in Wordsworth's poem," I remarked.

It was astonishing how this really rather good joke fell flat. Of course the twins did not see it. But Mrs. Vernon herself did not see it, and I too thought it, at the moment, inexpressibly feeble. As for the twins they could not hide their disappointment. Always before, I had handed them a little parcel, immediately, either at the station if they came to meet me, or at the house-door, if they did not. And to-day I had no little parcel. I could perceive that they were hoping against hope, even yet. I could perceive that they were saying to each other with their large, expressive eyes: "Perhaps he has put it in his portmanteau this time. He can't have forgotten us."

I could have wept for them. (I was in that state.) But I could not for the life of me tell them outright that I had forgotten the customary gift, and that I should send it by post on my return. No, I could not do that. I was too constrained, too ill at ease. So we all climbed up into the dog-cart. Mrs. Vernon and I in front, and the twins behind with the portmanteau to make weight; and the white mare set off with a bound, and the Dalmatian barked joyously, and we all pretended to be as joyous as the dog.

"Where's Jack?" I inquired.

"Oh!" said Mrs. Vernon, as though I had startled her. "He had to go to Bedbury Sands to look at a couple of greyhounds—it would have been too late on Monday. I'm afraid he won't be back for tea."

I guessed instantly that, with the average man's cowardice, he had run away in order to escape meeting me as I entered the house. He had left that to his wife. No doubt he hoped that by the time he returned I should have settled down and the first awkwardness and constraint would be past.

We said scarcely anything else, Mrs. Vernon and I, during the three-mile drive. And it was in silence that we crossed the portal of the house. Instead of having tea in the orchard we had it in the drawing-room, the twins being present. And the tea might have been a funeral feast.

"Well," I thought, "I anticipated a certain mutual diffidence, but nothing so bad as this. If they couldn't be brighter than this, why in heaven's name did they force me to come down?"

Mrs. Vernon was decidedly in a pitiable condition. She felt for me so much that I felt for her.

"Come along, dears," she said to the twins, after tea was over, and the tea-things cleared away. And she took the children out of the room. But before leaving she handed me a note, in silence. I opened it and read: "Be as kind to her as you can; she has suffered a great deal."

Then, ere I had time to think, the door, which Mrs. Vernon had softly closed, was softly opened, and a woman entered. It was Lucy, once Lucy Wren. She was as beautiful as ever, and no older. But her face was the face of one who had learnt the meaning of life. Till that moment I had sought everywhere for reasons to condemn her conduct towards me, to intensify its wickedness. Now, suddenly, I began to seek everywhere for reasons to excuse her. She had been so young, so guileless, so ignorant. I had been too stern for her. I had frightened her. How could she be expected to know that the man who had supplanted me was worthless? She had acted as she did partly from youthful foolishness and partly from timidity. She had been in a quandary. She had lost her head. And so it had occurred that one night, that night in August, she had kissed me falsely, with a lie on her lips, knowing that her jilting letter was already in the post. What pangs she must have experienced then! Yes, as she entered the room and gazed at me with her blue eyes, my heart overflowed with genuine sorrow for her.

"Lucy!" I murmured, "you are in mourning!"

"Yes," she said. "Didn't you know? Has Mrs. Vernon said nothing? He is dead."

And she sank down by the side of my chair and hid her face, and I could only see her honey-coloured hair. I stroked it. I knew all her history, in that supreme moment, without a word of explanation. I knew that she had been self-deceived, that she had been through many an agony, that she had always loved me. . . . And she was so young, so young.

I kissed her hair.

"How thankful I am!" breathed Mrs. Vernon afterwards. "Suppose it had not turned out well!"

Jack Vernon had calculated with some skill. When he came back, the constraint, the diffidence, was at an end.

A Dinner at the Louvre

The real name of this renowned West-End restaurant is not the Louvre. I have christened it so because the title seems to me to suit it very nicely, and because a certain disguise is essential. The proprietors of the Louvre—it belongs to an esteemed firm of caterers—would decidedly object to the coupling of the name of their principal establishment with an affair so curious and disconcerting as that which I am about to relate. And their objection would be perfectly justifiable. Nevertheless, the following story is a true one, and the details of it are familiar to at least half a dozen persons whose business it is, for one reason or another, to keep an eye upon that world of crime and pleasure, which is bounded on the east by Bow Street and on the left by Hyde Park Corner.

It was on an evening in the last week of May that I asked Rosie Mardon to dine with me at the Louvre. I selected the Louvre, well knowing that from some mysterious cause all popular actresses prefer the Louvre to other restaurants, although the quality of the food there is not always impeccable. I am not in the habit of inviting the favourites of the stage to dinner, especially favourites who enjoy a salary of seventy-five pounds a week, as Rosie Mardon did and does. But in the present case I had a particular object in view. Rosie Mardon was taking the chief feminine role in my new light comedy, then in active rehearsal at the Alcazar Theatre in Shaftesbury Avenue. We had almost quarrelled over her interpretation of the big scene in the second act, which differed materially from my own idea of how the scene ought to go. Diplomacy was necessary. I prided myself on my powers as a diplomatist: I knew that if I could chat with Miss Rosie in the privacy of a table for two at a public restaurant (there is no privacy more discreet), I could convert her to my opinions on that second act.

"Have you engaged a table upstairs?" was her first inquiry, as with the assistance of a stout and gorgeous official I helped her to alight from her brougham at the portico of the house. (She looked lovely, and half the street was envying me; but unfortunately Rosie's looks have nothing to do with the tale; let me therefore dismiss them as a dangerous topic.)

"No," I said; "but I expect there'll be plenty of room."

"Plenty of room!" she exclaimed, with a charming scorn and a glance which said: This young man really has a great deal to learn about the art of entertaining ladies at the Louvre." I admit that I had.

"Oh, yes!" I insisted with bravado. "Plenty!"

"Ask the booking-clerk," she commanded, and with all her inimitable grace she sank like a fatigued sylph into one of the easy-chairs that furnished the entrance-hall, and drew her cloak round her shoulders.

The booking-clerk, in faultless evening-dress, with a formidable silver chain encircling his neck, stood at the foot of the grand staircase, which was very grand. The booking-clerk politely but coldly informed me that he had not a table upstairs; he said that every table had been booked since a quarter to seven.

"Well, I suppose we must be content with downstairs, but I much prefer the balcony," said Rosie when I told her. And Rosie was obviously cross. My dinner was beginning ominously.

I returned to the booking-clerk, who was then good enough to tell me that he had no table downstairs either. I felt rather an ass, but never permit my asininity to go too far. I assumed an attitude of martial decision, and ordered one of the pages to get me a hansom.

"We will dine at the Savoy," I said, very loud. Every official in the neighbourhood heard me.

Rosie smiled, whether at the prospect of the Savoy or at my superb indignation I know not.

Just as we were emerging into the street the booking-clerk, his silver chain clinking, touched me on the shoulder.

"I can let you have a table upstairs now, sir," said he. "A party that engaged one has not arrived."

"I thought they wouldn't let us run away to the Savoy," I remarked to Rosie *sotto voce* and with satisfaction. I had triumphed, and the pretty creature was a witness of my triumph.

"What name, sir?" asked the clerk.

"John Delf," I replied.

His gesture showed that he recognised that name, and this pleased me too. Had not my first farcical comedy run a hundred and sixty nights at the Alcazar? It was only proper that my reputation should have reached even the clerks of restaurants. Another official recognised Miss Rosie's much-photographed face, and we passed up the staircase with considerable eclat.

"You managed that rather well," said Miss Rosie, dimpling with satisfaction, as we sat down in the balcony of the Grand Hall of the Louvre. The dinner was not beginning so ominously after all.

I narrate these preliminary incidents to show how large a part is played by pure chance in the gravest events of our lives.

I ordered the ten-and-sixpenny dinner. Who could offer to the unique Rosie Mardon a five-shilling or a seven-and-sixpenny repast when one at half-a-guinea was to be obtained? Not I! The meal started with anchovies, which Rosie said she adored. (She also adored nougat, crime de menthe, and other pagan gods.) As Rosie put the first bit of anchovy into her adorable mouth, the Yellow Hungarian Band at the other end of the crowded hall struck up the Rakocsy March, and the whole place was filled with clamour. Why people insist on deafening music as an accompaniment to the business of eating I cannot imagine. Personally, I like to eat in peace and quietude. But I fear I am an exception. Rosie's eyes sparkled with pleasure at the sound of the band, and I judged the moment opportune to ascertain her wishes on the subject of wine. She stated them in her own imperious way, and I signalled to the waiter.

Now I had precisely noticed, or I fancied I noticed, an extraordinary obsequiousness in this waiter—an obsequiousness surpassing the usual obsequiousness of waiters. I object to it, and my attitude of antagonism naturally served to intensify it.

"What's the matter with the fellow?" I said to Rosie after I had ordered the wine.

"He's very good-looking, isn't he?" was her only reply, as she gazed absently at the floor below us crowded with elegant diners.

And the waiter was indeed somewhat handsome. A light-haired man, and, like all the waiters at the Louvre, a foreigner with a deficient knowledge of English.

"I expect he's lost on his bets to-day," Rosie added. "They all bet, you know, and he's after a rousing tip to make up."

"Oh, is that it?" I said, wondering at the pretty creature's knowledge of the world. And then I began to talk about my play in my best diplomatic manner, inwardly chafing at the interruption of that weird Yellow Hungarian orchestra, which with bitter irony had hung over the railings of its stand a placard bearing the words, "By desire."

The meal proceeded brilliantly. My diplomacy was a success. The champagne was a success. We arrived at the sorbet, that icy and sweet product which in these days of enormous repasts is placed half-way through the meal in order to renew one's appetite for the second half. Your modern chef is the cruel tyrant of the stomach, and shows no mercy.

The fair-haired waiter's hand distinctly trembled as he served the sorbets. I looked at mine for some moments, hesitating whether or not to venture upon it. I am a martyr to indigestion.

"It's delicious," said Rosie. "More delicious than the second act of your 'Partners.'"

"Then I must risk it," I replied, and plunged the spoon into the half-frozen greenish mass. As I did so I caught sight of our waiter, who was leaning against the service table at the corner of the balcony. His face was as white as a sheet. I thought he must be ill, and I felt sorry for him. However, I began to swallow the sorbet, and the sorbet was in truth rather choice. Presently our waiter clutched at the sleeve of another waiter who was passing, and whispered a few words in his ear. The second waiter turned to look at me, and replied. Then our waiter almost ran towards our table.

"Excuse me, sirr," he murmured indistinctly, rolling the "r." "Are you not Count Vandernoff?"

"I am not," I replied briefly.

He hesitated; his hand wavered towards the sorbet, but he withdrew it and departed.

"Mon Dieu!" I heard him exclaim weakly under his breath.

"Possibly he's been taking me for an aristocratic compatriot of his own," I said to Rosie, "and that explains the obsequiousness. You were wrong about the betting."

I laughed, but I felt ill at ease, and to cover my self-consciousness I went on eating the sorbet very slowly.

I must have consumed nearly a third of it when I became conscious of a movement behind me; a mysterious hand shot out and snatched away the sorbet.

"Sir!" I protested, looking round. A tall, youngish man in evening dress, but wearing his hat, stood on my left. "Sir! what in the name of—?"

"Your pardon!" answered the man in a low hurried voice. I could not guess his nationality. "Let me beg you to leave here at once, and come with me."

"I shall do no such thing," I replied. "Waiter—call the manager." But our waiter had disappeared.

"It is a matter of life and death," said the man.

"To whom?"

"To you."

The man removed his hat and looked appealingly at Miss Rosie.

"Don't let's have a scene in here," said Rosie, with her worldly wisdom. And, impelled by the utter seriousness of the man, we went out. I forgot the bill, and no one presented it.

"I solemnly ask you to take a little drive with me," said the man, when we had reached the foyer. "I have a carriage at the door."

"Again, why?" I demanded.

He whispered: "You are poisoned. I am saving your life. I rely on your discretion."

My spine turned chilly, and I glanced at Miss Rosie. "I will come with you," she said.

In five minutes we had driven to a large house in Golden Square. We were ushered into a lavishly-furnished drawing-room, and we sat down. Rosie's lips were set. I admired her demeanour during those moments.

The man who said he was saving my life poured some liquid from a phial into a glass, and handed it to me.

"Emetics are useless. Drink this. In an hour you will feel the first symptoms of illness. They may be severe, though that is improbable, since you ate only a portion of the stuff. In any event, they will not last. To-morrow you will be perfectly well. Let me advise you to go to bed at once. My carriage is at your service and the service of this lady." He bowed.

I drank the antidote.

"Thanks for all these surprises," I said coldly. "But does it not occur to you that some explanation is due to me?"

He pondered a minute.

"I will explain," he replied. "It is your right. I will explain in two words. You have heard of Count Vandernoff, attached to the Russian Embassy in London? You may have seen in the papers that the Count has been appointed by the Tsar to be the new governor of Helsingfors, the Finnish capital?"

I nodded.

"You are aware," he continued suavely, "of the widespread persecutions in Finland, the taking away of the Constitution, the Russianising of all offices, the censorship of the Press? This persecution has given rise to a secret society, which I will call the Friends of Finnish Freedom. Its methods are drastic. Count Vandernoff was known to be violently antagonistic to Finnish freedom. He dines often at the Louvre. He had engaged a table for to-night. The waiter in charge of that table was, like myself, a member of the society, but, unfortunately, rather a raw hand. The Count, quite unexpectedly, did not arrive at the Louvre to-night. The waiter, however, took you for the Count. The sorbet which I snatched out of your hand was— Need I say more?"

"Poisoned?"

"Poisoned. The affair was carefully arranged, and only a pure accident could have upset it. That accident occurred."

"What was it?"

"The Count's coupe was knocked over by an omnibus in Piccadilly two hours ago, and the Count was killed."

There was a pause.

"Then he will never be governor of Helsingfors," I said.

"Heaven helps the right!" the man answered. "You English love freedom. You cannot guess what we in Finland have suffered. Let me repeat that I rely on your discretion."

We left, Miss Rosie and I; and the kind-hearted girl delivered me safely into the hands of my housekeeper. I was ill, but I soon recovered.

A few days later I met Miss Rosie at rehearsal.

"Did you notice?" she said to me, with an awed air, "our table was No. 13 that night."

Coachwhip Publications

CoachwhipBooks.com

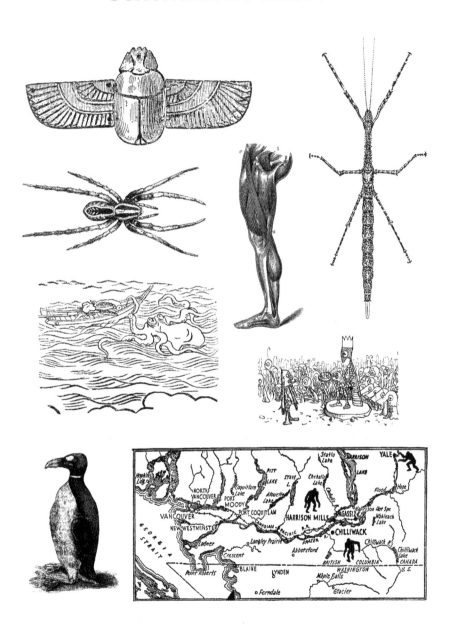

NOVEMBER JOE

DETECTIVE OF THE WOODS

H. HESKETH-PRICHARD

NOVEMBER JOE

ISBN 1-61646-013-X

THE PROBLEMIST: THORNLEY COLTON

ISBN 1-61646-017-2

AN AFRICAN MILLIONAIRE

ISBN 1-61646-014-8

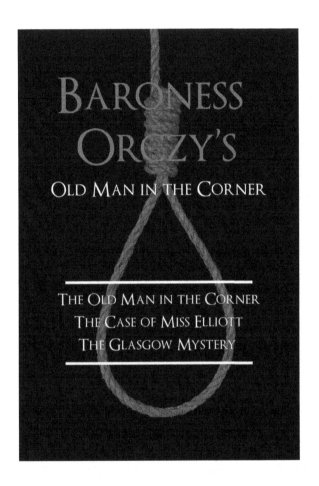

BARONESS ORCZY`S OLD MAN IN THE CORNER

ISBN 1-61646-015-6

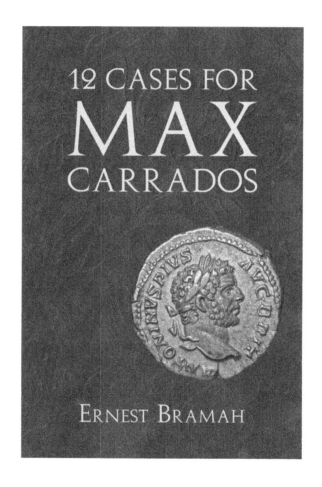

12 CASES FOR MAX CARRADOS

ISBN 1-61646-014-8

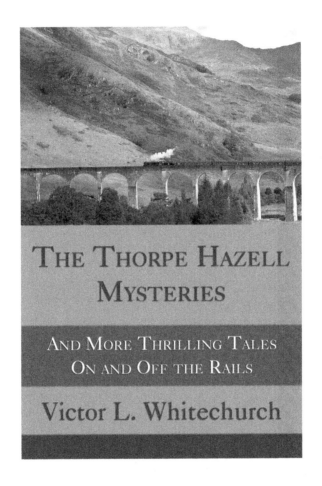

THE THORPE HAZELL MYSTERIES

ISBN 1-61646-018-0

Lightning Source UK Ltd.
Milton Keynes UK
UKOW04f2231031217
313808UK00001B/239/P

9 781616 460600